BEATING THE WRAP

JULIE ANNE LINDSEY

Cozy Queen
PUBLISHING

Dedicated to my Cozy Queens

A NOTE FROM THE AUTHOR

Hello Lovely Reader,

Thank you so much for joining me on Bonnie & Clyde's newest adventure! I hope you're having as much fun in Bliss as I am.

As you know, there will be eight novels in the Bonnie & Clyde Mysteries, along with additional, spin-off series, as secondary characters rise to the front and insist their stories be told. So, if you have a favorite, be sure to let me know!

You can keep in touch between the books via my Cozy Club newsletter.

And if you enjoy BEATING THE WRAP, don't forget to grab your copy of Eyelet Witness.

Now, let's go check in with your favorite furry little outlaw!
   -Julie Anne Lindsey

CHAPTER ONE

"Ow!" I shook my hand out at the wrist, then peered at my stinging fingertip.

Stringing popcorn was nothing like sewing, and absolutely not for the faint of heart, or thin of skin. I'd stabbed myself three times in five minutes and had eaten more of the popcorn than I'd strung.

I stuck my throbbing wound in my mouth and frowned.

"It's too bad Halloween was over two weeks ago, Bonnie," Lexi, my teenaged shopkeep said. "Your décor will look like a crime scene in no time if you keep that up."

I freed my fingertip and went back to work, determined to be more careful with my festive fall décor. And my bloodthirsty needle. I hoped the hint of Christmas would increase the appeal of an already inviting setup.

Lexi dragged long dark hair over one shoulder and fussed with the fringe of thick bangs across her forehead. She'd graduated from the local high school last summer and volunteered at Bless Her Heart to pay for her senior prom dress. It hadn't taken me long to realize she was a perfect fit for the store, and I hired her on a permanent basis.

My wild red hair had never been long or sleek enough to toss like hers without looking silly.

"Don't look now," she said. "But your furry little outlaw is on the hunt again."

I slid my narrowed gaze to the sleek black cat in my periphery.

Clyde hunkered beneath a row of sequined ball gowns. The holiday party attire display at the back of Bless Her Heart, my second-chance shop, was one of his many hiding spots. He did his best hunting from there. Usually he made off with things shoppers dropped, like gum wrappers, loose buttons or unsecured earrings, but currently, he wanted my popcorn.

I wasn't sure if he ate the fallen pieces or just hid them, but so far he'd taken seven.

"I appreciate his dedication," Lexi said, carrying a basket of stuffed pumpkins to the cozy sitting area outside my shop's dressing rooms. "Every store should have a mascot." She arranged the velvet and crocheted items on a glass-and-brass coffee table set between a pair of cream-and-taupe armchairs, then stepped back to admire her work. "What do you think?"

"I love it, as always," I said. "You've got a natural talent for decorating."

She smiled. "And you have a talent for doing all of this." She opened her arms as if she might twirl but settled for motioning around the shop.

I let my gaze roam and admire the space around us. I'd turned the old bank space, which had previously held a row of tellers' workstations, stanchions with velvet ropes and a few desks, into something lovely, where clothing and furniture that otherwise might have been consigned to the trash heap instead were refurbished and given a second chance with new owners.

My shop was rectangular. A substantial shop window stood beside a glass front door, with beautiful views of the town square across the street. A large circular checkout counter stood at the center of the shop, several paces inside the door. Small displays of housewares and décor polka-dotted the space around the desk. Bookcases lined most of the rear wall, and racks of clothing stood along one side. The entry to a rear hallway with a restroom and office opened on the other. A set of changing rooms were tucked into the corner, and I'd gathered refinished furniture sets into mini-scenes here and there. I kept a refreshments table beside the register and encouraged shoppers to grab something sweet while they browsed, maybe have a seat on one of the chairs and see how much they'd like to take it home as well.

My throat thickened a bit with the emotion that always came when I remembered how incredibly blessed I was and how grateful I was for the opportunity to start over in Bliss. "Thank you."

I'd opened Bless Her Heart last spring, after my husband of nearly twenty years filed for divorce. At first, it'd been rough to accept the end of something I'd worked, single-handedly, for so long to save, but returning to my hometown of Bliss, Georgia, had been the right move. In hindsight, it was probably the best thing that could've happened, even if I hadn't realized it at the time.

I'd grown up on a flower farm about six miles from the shop, and I'd learned early to find beauty in everything. Also, how to stretch a shoestring budget to its limits. Then just a little more. Bless Her Heart paid homage to all that.

Even the most struggling paupers could dress and decorate like a queen if they shopped at Bless Her Heart. Because everyone deserved to feel beautiful and worthy of fabulous things.

Clyde wiggled his backside, winding up to pounce as I

worked my needle against another salty treat. His bowtie was golden today, and didn't match my ensemble as much as coordinate in spirit, as we'd both chosen fall colors. Also, the bowtie didn't have a bell, which pleased him. I supposed the lack thereof made him feel more like the kitty ninja he aspired to be.

I concentrated on the needle, afraid of sticking myself yet again. The small white puffed corn fell, and a streak of black darted from beneath the dresses. He'd zoomed across my feet before I could protest or get out of the way.

Then, like magic, both my cat and the treat were gone.

Lexi snorted softly as she smiled her way back to the counter. "I don't understand how he doesn't weigh fifty pounds."

"That's easy," I said. "He burns off all the extra calories every time I open the door and he darts outside. He runs around out there doing who-knows-what until he deems it time to grace me with his presence again."

"When he gets hungry," she said.

"Exactly."

Lexi sorted through the box of carefully curated throw pillows and blankets behind the counter while I strung another piece of popcorn without injury. She gathered a selection, in a variety of textures, then carried them around the shop in search of the perfect places to display them.

Typically, the store was decked out in pastels, whites and soft grays. From October 1st through Thanksgiving, however, my shop was a cornucopia of vibrant autumn shades. From amber to scarlet, eggplant to gold, and everything in between. A visual celebration of the bounty that was harvest season in our beloved farming community.

She admired the rows of twinkle lights woven among the tomes and trinkets on bookcases, loose jingle bells strategically placed here and there. "I don't know, Bonnie," she said.

"I think we have a good chance of winning the decorating contest. Too many of the other shops have gone straight to Christmas with their concepts, but the rules say this is a celebration of autumn. You've nailed autumn. Christmas is a whole other animal." She delivered the blankets and pillows to their new destinations, then returned to me once more.

"It's not supposed to be Christmas decorating, but everyone loves that look," I said. "My guess is that the rules won't matter when it comes time to vote."

Lexi swiped a piece of popcorn from my bowl, then eyeballed my finger and frowned. She returned the popcorn. "Do you think many people will vote?"

"I do. Cami's arranged a couple of events this week to get people to the square. Once folks are here, I think they'll be glad to cast their vote on the best looking storefront."

My best friend, Cami, was the chairwoman for a beautification program sweeping downtown. She'd taken on the monumental task of sprucing up a long forgotten area, then enticing shoppers far and wide to come and check us out. Given that Bliss was a solid hour's drive from the nearest highway or major town, and our citizens had a long history of *not* coming downtown, she'd had her work cut out for her.

Lexi smiled in quiet awe. "I love her. She was asked to convince folks to shop downtown and she's reuniting the whole community in the process."

"Things do look really good in here," I said, feeling a rush of pride. "And the window display is perfect. I have plans for the sidewalk stuff too." I didn't want to make a big deal out of it to Lexi, but I was feeling more than a little competitive about who had the prettiest storefront.

The prize was a window decal announcing the store as winner for the year. There was a gift basket too, which included one item from each participating shop, but I was most interested in the bragging rights. I wanted every good thing for my store, and I wanted everyone who walked by to know it was wonderful.

"I think we've got a good shot at the win," Lexi said, a proud smile on her youthful face.

I smiled at Lexi, hoping she couldn't see how bad I wanted to beat the figurative pants off of all the other shops. "I hope you're right."

"I am," she said. "The only other place that's done half this much decorating is The Truck Stop."

I frowned, despite myself. The retail space across the square, previously known as Gnome Alone, had closed several months ago. In its place was The Truck Stop, which sold home décor as well, but instead of whimsical pointy hats and gnomes, this theme was old farm trucks. I'd never met the owner, but I knew who he was. I guessed him to be in his late fifties, tall and lean with mostly gray hair and a perpetual five o'clock shadow. He rarely smiled and never spoke. He didn't attend any of Cami's events and couldn't be bothered to join the rest of the shop owners on shop hop nights, when we all stayed open an extra hour or two and offered special sales to those who came to shop after dark. I definitely didn't want that guy to win. "Have you been to that store?" I asked, trying to look more casual than I felt.

Lexi rolled her eyes. "If I ever spend fifty dollars on a hand-carved cutting board or buy a welcome mat featuring a truck full of pumpkins, just haul me to nearest shrink because I've finally gone around the bend."

I smiled, wondering who the nearest shrink might be. I'd had a couple scary encounters in the past year, and wouldn't mind telling someone, professionally, about how the experiences lingered in my mind and seemed to cling to my skin some days. Or how, when the residual fear hit, it usually came without warning.

"I'm going to do the gratitude tags now," she said.

I finished loading my string with popcorn while Lexi arranged a calligraphy set and a stack of oversized cardstock gifts tags onto the counter. She'd outlined each tag in golden glitter last week and strung red ribbon through holes at their tops. Now, adding them to our window display was part of her workday routine.

The tags were part of my Gifts of Gratitude campaign.

I'd wrapped a large square box in red paper and tied it with a golden bow, then cut a small slot in the box's top and set it on a table outside my shop's door. I kept a selection of pens and papers on the table beside the giant gift, with a note encouraging folks to take a minute from their days to leave a nice note about someone or something in the community.

Lexi transcribed the messages onto the pretty, pre-glittered notes and hung them in our window display.

"Be right back," she said, heading for the shop's front door.

A set of sleighbells I'd tied to the top jingled as she hurried onto the sidewalk, then unlidded the box.

I held my breath a little. The notes also weren't always nice, and I hated that.

Especially since those particular messages were usually about me.

Lexi did not transcribe those and hang them in my window.

Zero gratitude for Ms. Balfour.

Not thankful for this shop's owner.

"Aww," Lexi said, slipping back inside with the contents of the gratitude box. "Anonymous is thankful your store made the wedding of her dreams possible." She turned the card to face me. "And this is just a crayon drawing of a turkey. Oh my goodness. How sweet." She passed both papers to me, and my heart melted a little at the compliment and the turkey. "This place is changing lives," Lexi said. "One wedding, prom and heart at a time." She flipped through the rest of the stack, smiling, then spread the messages on the counter to transfer to the tags.

I went in search of the perfect frame to showcase my turkey.

Maybe the vague written attacks on my character had come to an end and my luck was turning. I felt my shoulders relax and my smile lift at that possibility.

Lexi carried a set of finished tags to the window display and climbed inside, arranging the new notes of gratitude on the garlands of greenery hanging along the ceiling and down the sides.

Movement outside the shop door caught my eye, and I craned my neck for a better look. "I think someone is drop-ping another note into the box," I said. "I'm so glad this idea caught on." I'd worried no one would take the time to stop and leave a kind word with the holidays looming and the days racing away.

"Me too," Lexi said. "I think this is going to cinch your win." She dusted together her palms and grinned. "What are you adding to the winner's basket?"

Each participating shop donated a prize for the basket. I'd gone the simplistic route. "I'm giving a gift certificate to the store and one of Gigi's pies." Gigi was my grandma and hands down the best baker in town. Choosing an item from my store had seemed presumptuous. A certificate was the better choice. Plus, it would cause the winner to visit Bless Her Heart and take a look for themselves. Hopefully they'd also fall in love with the merchandise and keep coming back when the need for upcycled clothing or home goods presented itself. I'd used a similar thought process when adding one of Gigi's pies. She was opening a bakery soon, so if the winner loved what they got with the basket, maybe they'd stop by her shop when it opened and buy another.

Lexi nodded. "Smart. I wonder if Gretchen will give away a free soul mate reading. I'd kill for one of those." Her eyes went dreamy at the mention of our friend Gretchen and her alleged ability to tell anyone who their soul mate is and when or if they'll meet. People came from far and wide to Gretchen's Golden Matches shop to talk about love, and they paid a pretty penny for her time. I'd been sidestepping her good-natured desire to tell me about my love life for free for months. If she'd spent nineteen years in the same marriage I had, she'd understand.

"Well," I said, feeling Lexi's youthful, unjaded hope vibrating across the room. "If we win the decorating competition, and Gretchen includes a free soul mate reading, you can have it. How about that?"

Lexi made a sharp squealing sound and smiled maniacally.

"You're welcome," I said with a laugh.

"Speaking of love," Lexi said. "How's the HANS?"

I rolled my eyes. Local ladies had begun referring to my friend Mason Wright as the HANS, an acronym for Handsome New Sheriff. They weren't wrong, but the nickname wasn't as stealthy as anyone thought. Mason knew exactly what it meant. I still giggled at the recollection of his expression when I told him.

"He's fine," I said. "Grumpy as always. A little too northern for his own good, but that's just fun for me." Watching the Cleveland, Ohio, native try to understand some of the old timers and make sense of our general southernness was fantastic entertainment. I smiled at the thought. Five stars. Highly recommend.

Mason was a homicide detective in his former life. He'd

had a tough time after an undercover operation went sideways, and he came to Bliss to get his head straight. The old sheriff talked him into staying, and an election earlier this fall confirmed his placement. Everyone loved Mason. The jury was out on what he thought of everyone else.

Motion outside caught my eye again. This time, I stepped toward the window as a man in a tan windbreaker moved swiftly down the sidewalk, away from my store. "I think there's a new note. I'll get it."

I stepped outside and Clyde darted past my feet, then crouched under a car parked at the curb.

I glared at my cat a moment, then sighed. Clyde was a furry little Houdini and former alley cat, who did what he wanted and dared me to try and stop him. So far I had not been able to do so.

I moved my focus back to the box. I removed the lid and the single slip of folded paper inside.

Lexi opened the door, palm out. "I'll transfer it now. All my supplies are still on the counter."

"I think it was that man from The Truck Stop," I said, staring in the direction the man had gone.

Could I have misjudged him? Was he just a little shy?

Lexi dropped her hand to her side and frowned. "Weird. We were just talking about him." She held the door open while we went back inside. "What's the paper say?"

I unfolded the note and frowned at the hurried scrawl.

I'M GRATEFUL MS. BALFOUR DOESN'T HAVE MORE ANIMALS.

Yeah. He definitely didn't like me.

CHAPTER TWO

"See," I told Lexi, passing her the slip. "Mean. Just like I said." I marched behind the counter and opened a small jewelry box, where I'd kept all the other vaguely rude notes. "Here. See if the handwriting matches. I'll bet they're all from him."

"You kept all the mean notes?"

I pushed them in her direction, lips pursed.

She smiled. "Of course you did. Let me see." She looked at each note carefully, then back to me. "You didn't actually see him put this note in the box," she said. "You might've seen him walking away from Blissful Bean next door. The person who wrote these could've been anyone else out there."

I took the notes from her fingers and looked through them again. "All perfect matches."

"I can't believe you kept them," Lexi said. "Why would you do that?"

An excellent question, but I didn't want to look too closely at the answer. "Can you watch the store?"

"Bonnie," Lexi said, hurrying toward the door. "Where are you going?"

I went to the refreshments table. "I'm going to ask Mr. Truck Stop if he wrote all of these mean things. If I can identify the problem, I can fix it."

She shook her head but maintained her position as a roadblock. "You can't accuse an old man of anything. You're the one who will wind up looking like the bully."

"I'll ask politely," I said, adding four pecan sandies to a small plastic sleeve. I'd made a double batch last night while trying to choose the right tile for my kitchen backsplash. The decision felt too permanent. I didn't want to choose wrong and be stuck with something I didn't like, or that wrecked my overall design effect, for years to come. Baking helped me untangle my thoughts. It also tightened my pants, so I brought the goodies to work with me every day and did my best to get them into other people's hands.

"No confrontations," Lexi said. "Even with cupcakes."

She was right, but I still wanted answers. "I'm taking cookies."

Lexi made the sort of sarcastic expression only teenage girls could manage.

I tied the bag with ribbon and grabbed a pair of napkins. I needed to know if this was the man who didn't like me, and if there was a reason for it, I wanted to know why. I was a fixer by nature, and this was a serious problem for me.

"I promise not to confront him," I said. "I'll go under the guise of delivering these delicious cookies, then I'll look for something he wrote and see if the handwriting matches the notes."

I moved to stand before her, a saccharine smile on my lips.

Lexi exhaled deeply and dropped her arms. "Don't say I didn't warn you."

"Be back soon," I said.

No one could stay mad at me if I came bearing sweets.

I was counting on it.

I hurried down the sidewalk to the crosswalk, pecan sandies in hand and unappreciated notes in my pocket. I'd spent years being a human doormat in Atlanta, and not just for my husband. I'd learned early the best way for a house-wife from a farming community to fit into the high-class world of career-driven wealthy folks was to be quiet, look pretty, and cause zero trouble, lest the ones originally from that world band together and crush me. It had only taken one well-intended suggestion during a corporate fund-drive planning session to turn my new friends against me. That had been in year one of my marriage. After that, I'd kept my mouth shut and baked away all thoughts of injustice.

Being back home was supposed to be about finding myself, even if that meant standing out from time to time, in good ways, and never blending in for someone else's comfort at the expense of my own.

So, if I'd somehow upset another shop owner in town, I wanted to know why so I could fix it or at least apologize and move on.

Clyde trotted along before me, then jumped onto the narrow exterior window ledge at the bookstore. He positioned himself between a basket of gourds and a pint-sized stuffed scarecrow and peered inside.

I waved as I passed, in case the store's owner, Liz, was watching. The window's smokey old glass made it difficult to see beyond the piles of books inside.

The streetlight changed, and I speed walked to the opposite sidewalk, then onto the lush green grass of our town square. The square was actually a large oval, peppered in majestic, mossy oaks and anchored by a large octagonal gazebo on one end. Thanks to Cami's efforts, the structure was now ringed in baskets of brightly colored mums. And flags with the *Shop Bliss!* logo hung from streetlamps around the square.

I cut to the path that curved lazily through the center, past park benches and large twisted metal art displays, courtesy of the local gallery.

I smiled and waved at familiar faces, chasing little ones and walking dogs, before landing, a little sweatier, on the opposite sidewalk, then dashed across the next road to my destination.

The Truck Stop's storefront was trimmed in white with a hand-painted sign above the shop window bearing the name. An unfinished arrangement of model buildings, trucks and trees was set up in the dark mulch between the sidewalk and storefront. The owner was apparently recreating the town square piece by piece. Except in his rendition, everyone drove an old farm truck.

A man's fairy garden.

I rolled my eyes and grabbed the small wrought iron handrail beside the single cement step to the door.

Inside, music from an era as far past as the celebrated trucks bopped softly through the air. Tables of roughhewn wood lined the walls, and a massive wooden spool like those used by utility companies for running wires sat at the store's center. A nice touch, I had to admit.

The floors were high polished and mahogany stained. Faux wood beams lined the ceiling, adding to the rustic atmosphere, and every flat surface was covered in décor featuring old farm trucks with bulbous fenders, seasonal loads and messages down their sides. *Welcome, Good Old Days*, and *Happy Holidays*, seemed to be the most common.

He'd secured an old-fashioned gas pump in the window display and large metal signs from various motor companies and advertisers of all things truck-related adorned the walls.

The man, whose name I couldn't recall, watched me suspiciously as he spoke quietly with a customer.

I eyeballed the script on paper price tags, straining to determine if he was in fact the man who left me so many mean-spirited notes. The numbers weren't enough to make a judgment.

"Excuse me," someone said, reaching past me to take the small blue truck filled with miniature hay bales.

I stepped aside to allow the woman easier access. "Certainly."

Behind me, the shop door opened and closed a half-dozen times, letting newcomers in and satisfied customers out, each with a large logoed bag.

I swung my attention back to the man, busy at the counter, then made my way in his direction.

"All hand-carved and painted," he told an elderly couple as he wrapped their new Welcome sign in brown paper, carefully taping the edges. "My dad and granddad were wood-carvers. I started out in sales and marketing, but eventually found my way back to my roots."

His tone was kind and congenial. His expression pleasant.

I bit my lip, a little uncertain. Had I been wrong about him? Perhaps I'd always noticed him at bad times, when he was scowling instead of smiling like he was now.

Maybe this wasn't the man who'd left passive aggressive notes in my Gifts of Gratitude box after all.

He slid his eyes to me as I craned my neck for a look at an order pad by his phone on the countertop.

I could be wrong about him, but I wouldn't know for sure until I had a look at his writing. I peeked at the note in my pocket, then back at the paper beside his register.

He was apparently meeting the Road Crew, whatever that was, tonight at a diner on the edge of town, and a surveyor in couple of days.

It took a long beat for the elongated S in surveyor to catch my eye. The same long, lazy, almost melting shape as the S's from my notes.

My eyes narrowed as I raised them to meet his stare.

The couple at the register had gone.

"Ms. Balfour," he said, expression clear as he soaked my name in disdain. "Something I can help you with?"

My arm shot forward in the only defense I had. The stack of cookies bagged in the festive plastic sleeve dangled from my fingertips. The gold-and-crimson ribbon tied pertly in a bow. "I don't think we've officially met. I thought I'd bring you a hello gift."

He took the offering. "Joe Fryer."

"Bonnie Balfour," I said, though he'd already addressed me by my last name. "You can call me Bonnie."

Mr. Fryer tugged the ribbon loose and shoved a cookie into his mouth, his bushy salt-and-pepper brows furrowed. "What really brings you around?" he asked, fishing a second cookie from the cellophane before he'd finished the first. "Some kind of local shop espionage?" He slid his gaze pointedly to the notes I'd been staring at. "What's in your pocket you kept looking at? Instructions of some kind?"

I wrinkled my nose at him. "No. They're notes," I said, freeing the papers in question and offering them to him on my palm. "From you."

A thrill of victory rushed through me as his stunned expression confirmed the truth. I was right, and I'd proved my theory. The jig was up. Now, the silent badgering could stop, and I could open my Gifts of Gratitude display without fearing what might be inside. "Well?" I prompted. "Do you think we should talk about these?"

Several shoppers blatantly turned to stare.

"I don't need an apology," I offered magnanimously. "But I

would like an explanation." Then, maybe, I could figure out what went wrong and fix it. Maybe Mr. Fryer would even like me after this was all cleared up.

Fryer's hand closed around the cookie bag, deforming the remaining contents. "An apology," he repeated, pale-blue eyes hard and a mass of wrinkles gathering over his forehead. "You think you can come over here with some so-so cookies and I'm going to tell you I'm sorry for speaking up against this town's little princess?"

I gaped. My cheeks heated and my stance went rigid. My cookies were absolutely not so-so, and I was looking down the barrel of a fortieth birthday. I hadn't been a princess in a very long time.

I imagined what I must look like from the outside, still and silent, despite my internal fury. Given my impossibly pale skin, red hair and hot blush climbing my chest, neck and face, I probably resembled a cartoon thermometer.

He dropped the bag of crushed cookies into the wastebasket, never breaking eye contact while I fumed.

I rolled my shoulders back and lifted my chin.

"You put mean notes in my Gifts of Gratitude display," I said flatly. "Why on earth would you do that? You don't even know me."

The shoppers inched closer, suddenly interested in items nearest Mr. Fryer and me.

He crossed his arms over the dark-blue work shirt with his name embroidered on the pocket. He cast his gaze around the room but didn't speak, presumably saving face with the shoppers and letting me become the bad guy.

"The problem with your notes," I said, careful to watch my tone but unable to stop myself from carrying on, "is that they're all incredibly rude and intentionally vague. How can I be expected to improve upon whatever it is that upset you enough to write them if you never come out and state the problem."

He glared.

I glared back. "What. Is. Your. Problem?"

His waning composure snapped, and he tipped forward, planting his palms on the counter between us. "I hate your cat."

A soft gasp rolled through the store, falling from eaves-droppers' lips, and I felt my palm against my collarbone, grasping for invisible pearls.

"My cat?" I asked, as appalled as I was shocked. "How dare you," I whispered, wishing I could get my cookies back. He didn't deserve them. And I wouldn't be able to make amends with an animal hater.

"I dare because you don't take care of him," Fryer snarled.

My jaw dropped impossibly further. "I love my cat," I said, suddenly so angry I feared I might cry. An unfortunate genetic condition linked the anger portion of my brain directly to my tear ducts, and I hated it, but there was nothing to be done. "Clyde is family," I seethed. "I treat him better than I treat myself some days."

Mr. Fryer snorted. "If that's what you consider good care, I hope you don't have children."

I batted my eyes rapidly, forcing back the brewing tears. He'd hit a hot button I hadn't expected. My infertility had been a sore spot in my marriage for years. Grant had built an empire and wanted an heir to pass it on to. I'd longed for a child to love and cherish, to teach and care for. So, we'd spent tens of thousands of dollars trying to conceive, trav-eled to all the best fertility specialists. I'd undergone multiple uncomfortable, sometimes painful, procedures, to no avail. And in the end, my spirit had been broken. Grant couldn't deal with the failure of our attempts, and he'd simply stopped touching me. In the years after, he'd slowly stopped speaking to me as well.

And Mr. Fryer had said the one thing that could send me back to that ugly, lonely, heartbroken place, in front of a dozen witnesses.

I reached for the counter to steady myself and willed my tears not to fall. I'd surely look like a nut, crying over such a seemingly simple set of words. I took a step toward the door, then another, forcing a smile that probably looked maniacal as I concentrated on my escape.

"That cat of yours," he said, heavy footfalls following after me, "has stolen half my town! My daddy and granddaddy made those pieces, and I displayed them outside to show folks the incredible woodworking talent in my family. Your cat comes over every morning and takes a piece!"

I pushed open the door and paused to inhale the warm morning air. My gaze fell to the small, unfinished town replica in the mulch. I'd assumed he was still setting up the scene. Instead, the pieces had been disappearing. Courtesy of Clyde.

That would be frustrating.

"Those pieces are special," Fryer said, holding open the door and standing on the step as I hurried to the sidewalk. "Those pieces mean something!"

A fresh group of meandering shoppers and locals turned as his voice boomed into the day.

"You let that cat run wild," he continued, "stealing and wreaking havoc. I ought to call animal control or the pound. If I ever catch him…"

I spun on my heels before Fryer could finish that sentence. My impending tears dried instantly, and my proverbial claws appeared. "You'll what?"

Fryer seemed to return to himself and notice the onlookers he'd caused.

My hands curled into fists at my sides, and I clenched my teeth, searching internally for the control I'd nearly lost. "Mr. Fryer," I said, plastering on my most southern of smiles. "I had no idea Clyde was taking your things. Now that I do, you can rest assured I'll do everything I can to make this right because I am a good neighbor and a nice person. But I love my cat, sir. He is my best friend, and he is family. So, you'd be wise not to threaten him again."

I turned to storm off dramatically as a flash of black fur caught my eye.

Clyde charged toward the miniature display, mouth open and paw stretched toward a small blue pickup.

"For Pete's sake," I muttered, bending to scoop my kitty from the mulch.

Then I hurried away as quickly as I could, eager to leave the mean man and rubbernecking crowd behind.

"You see!" Fryer cried, louder now, probably hoping I'd hear him and turn.

I imagined him shaking a fist in the air or sweeping an arm wide, as if to present the evidence of my awful cat ownership to the staring crowd.

But I refused to look back.

"Let me catch that cat stealing one more thing—" he said.

My feet anchored, and I spun on autopilot. "Do not finish that sentence or you will regret it."

Mr. Fryer straightened, apparently pleased by my reaction, and looking significantly braver than he had while I was still in reaching distance. "And it will be the last time he steals anything," he said slowly, enunciating each word.

The amassed spectators turned collectively in my direction, jaws open as they waited for my reaction.

One particular face stood out above the others. At six-foot-three, Sheriff Mason Wright was easy to spot in any crowd, and his trademark scowl said he'd already heard more than I would have preferred.

I gave Fryer one last murderous look, then turned for Bless Her Heart, where I planned to sit on the floor and cry out my frustration while feeding Clyde popcorn.

CHAPTER THREE

The rest of the day passed in a blur while Lexi ran the shop and I cleaned like a mad woman, paying specific and careful attention to the nooks and crannies. I wasn't convinced there would be much return for my invested effort when I'd started the mad search, crawling on my hands and knees to peek under clothing racks and behind refinished furniture for signs of Fryer's tiny town pieces. But I'd been wrong.

"It's seven o'clock," Lexi said. "Should I lock up?"

"Yeah." I pointed the flashlight app from my phone beneath a bookcase. "Let's call it a day."

Lexi made her way to the door and gave the deadbolt a twist.

The soft sound of her turning the window sign from OPEN to CLOSED came next.

"I was sure Gigi would be in today," she said, sounding more than a little disappointed.

Gigi was my mama's mama and my grandmama. A five-foot satchel of sass with graying red hair and mischievous hazel eyes. She was spunky and loud. Often unapologetic,

and I was sure our proper, well-mannered southern ances-
tors would have a word or two for her when they met again
one day. Until then, she was ours to enjoy.

I stretched onto my feet and dusted off my aching knees.
Getting on and off the floor was harder all the time, and it
made me want to get back in shape. But I didn't want it badly
enough to actually do it, which was depressing. I rolled my
shoulders and gripped the too-tight muscles along each side
of my back. "I'm sure we'll hear from her tomorrow."

Gigi and Lexi had bonded at my shop shortly after Gigi's
return to Bliss. I'd hired Lexi the same week, and the connection between them was instant—Gigi was impossible not to
love. She was negotiating the purchase of Blissful Bean, the
coffee shop next door. Once the deal's details were
hammered out, the plan was to renovate the shop to suit
Gigi's new bakery start-up needs. She wanted to install a
door in our adjoining wall so shoppers could move freely
between our spaces without going outside. I loved the idea of
joining our shops however we could, but I suspected the
health department would put a hard No on allowing a cat in
the bakery. So, adding a pretty set of etched glass doors
seemed the next best option.

Lexi peered through the window, possibly watching for
signs of Gigi. "Do you think she's going to make the deal?"

"Yeah," I said, smiling as I made my way to the counter.
"She and Dave have known one another for decades. He's
owned Blissful Bean for almost as long, and he was looking
for the right person to sell to last year. Gigi is that person. I
know it."

Plus, price wasn't an issue. Thanks to Mason's FBI friend
Dale, who could find a literal needle in a haystack, my
divorce settlement had resulted in half of Grant's hidden
millions. I was still getting my head around the amount.
Only my parents, Gigi, Cami, Dale and Mason knew I'd

come into so much money, and I intended to keep it that way. Money was a major issue in a farming community, and I planned to use mine to make differences.

Because of my settlement, Gigi could agree to whatever price Dave needed to retire and spend time with his daughter. And Gigi could embark on her new adventure without worrying how she could also afford to eat and not lose her house.

I set a small hand-carved wooden stop sign and tree on the countertop and sighed. Clyde had hidden a number of the stolen pieces from Mr. Fryer's town square replica in my shop. I wasn't sure how many were missing in total, but I'd found nine.

"It's so exciting," Lexi said, staring at the wall where a door would soon be. "Gigi's going to make a fortune with her cakes and pies. She's already everyone's favorite, and she's just selling from a tent on the square once a week."

I grinned. "Well, her goodies are unparalleled."

Lexi laughed. "Both my grandmamas passed when I was young. I love that she's so willing to be everyone's grandmama, friend, sister, whatever they need. And she's funny."

"Agreed." Gigi was hands down one of my favorite people, and she deserved the world. I was thrilled to help her get her new business started. "I'll get an update over breakfast tomorrow at my folks' place," I said. "I'll fill you in when I see you, but she's probably just been busy making rounds through town to celebrate."

Lexi nodded, but her smile waned. "Tell her I'm really excited for her."

Lexi was from a big family, but they weren't close like my family, and it was easy to forget how much our lives mattered to her. In some ways Gigi, my folks and I had become Lexi's family too.

"I will," I said gently. "But you can also tell her yourself. I know she'll be around as soon as she can."

My gaze dropped to the collection of figures I'd lined up on the countertop. Reclaimed from Clyde's stash.

"Did you find them all?" Lexi asked, staring at the pile of wooden pieces.

"I'm not sure. Fryer didn't say how many were gone, but this is probably a good start in building a bridge."

Clyde leaped onto the counter and sniffed the little display of stolen items.

Lexi laughed. "He looks like a giant. Take a picture!"

I laughed and snapped the shot, then took the clock tower from his mouth before he ran off with it again. The clock tower had been removed from the square long before I was born, but Mr. Fryer's dad or granddad had immortalized it in a tiny carving.

Lexi pulled a clear white bag with the Bless Her Heart logo from beneath the counter. "I'll bag them up before they vanish. You should probably add a note," she said, moving the pieces into the bag.

I frowned at the idea of writing something nice to him, when his unkind messages had been the things that started all this.

Lexi handed me a piece of paper and a pen.

"Fine." I pulled in a deep, cleansing breath and tried to find the desire to be a bigger person somewhere inside.

The glass front door rattled from a hearty knock, and I jumped.

"Gigi!" Lexi called, running to let my grandma inside. "How was the meeting?" she asked, tugging her in and ushering her to the tan-and-white upholstered chairs.

Gigi waved at me as she shuffled past, then obligingly took a seat.

Lexi rushed to the refreshments table and grabbed two

half-sized bottles of water from my mini-fridge, then hurried them back to the chairs and took the seat beside Gigi.

The women smiled at one another, and the contrast was both beautiful and drastic. Aside from the more than half century between them, Gigi was geriatric, pale and petite like me. Lexi was young, tan and athletic, with perfectly sculpted dark brows. Gigi had plucked her eyebrows to death long before I was born, and they'd never recovered, so she drew them on now. She kept her naturally twisty hair in a short, cropped style and frequently dyed it the color of a flame, which suited her.

She accepted the offered water with an appreciative smile, then began to unpack the details of her day.

I listened as she spoke with Lexi, enjoying the exchange between them while willfully ignoring the pen in my hand and paper beneath it.

"And that's it," Gigi finished. "Thanks to my granddaughter, her unfortunate marriage and overdue divorce, I get a bake shop."

Lexi giggled. "Nice."

I jerked my eyes in Gigi's direction, then let my attention move to Lexi. "That's all completely confidential information."

Lexi nodded, unable to squelch her smile. "No one will hear it from me."

I hoped that was true, and I was sure she meant it, but trust was admittedly not my strongest skill.

Gigi crossed her short legs and leaned forward on her seat, clasping her hands around one knee. "I hear you had quite a big day as well." She pumped her eyebrows at me. "Telling off that old turnip at The Truck Stop after he threatened Clyde."

I rolled my eyes. "I shouldn't have done that."

"I hear you really got his goat," she said. "He's lucky I

wasn't there. No one threatens our kitty."

Lexi beamed. "Bonnie's writing him an apology."

Gigi gaped. "What?" Her gaze fell to my pen and paper. "Why on earth would you do that? I heard he was the one leaving those mean messages."

"He was," Lexi said, sounding excessively scandalized. "Can you believe it?"

I sighed and scribbled the word *Sorry* on the paper, then stuffed it into the bag with the stolen figures and wooden pieces. "I found a bunch of the things Clyde stole from him, and I'm going to take them back before I go home."

Gigi stood. "I'd better go with you, in case he gives you any trouble."

I dropped the bag into my purse then set the kitty carrier on my counter. "I think this is something I'd better do alone," I said. "If he sees you coming, he might lock the door."

"What's that supposed to mean?" She lifted her chin and set her hands on her hips.

Lexi stood at her side. "I think she means your reputation precedes you."

Her short temper and big mouth preceded her, but I wasn't going to say that. Or mention that the last time she got all riled up, she tried to climb into a giant shoe to fight her nemesis. We both got thrown out of the Enchanted Gardens, and she became a murder suspect. That was just last summer.

"I've got this," I assured her. "Lock up when you go." I scooped a lounging Clyde out of the window display and stuffed him into his crate, then headed for the door with my things.

They waved their goodbyes and went back to chatting on the chairs.

Outside, the night was warm and beautiful. A band of periwinkle stretched across the horizon with deepening shades of blue and purple layered above. A few stars had made their appearance, but the silver hook of moon was barely visible in its newness.

Around the square, shopfronts were illuminated in festive twinkle lights and the seating areas outside cafes were dressed in zigzags of bobbing bistro bulbs. Streetlamps glowed golden above their corn stalk wrappings and hanging baskets of jewel-toned mums.

I set Clyde's carrier on the passenger seat of my new Volkswagen. The gently used T-Roc Cabriolet convertible wasn't anywhere near the price point of the BMW I'd considered my only friend before meeting Clyde, but she was a convertible, like her predecessor, and driving with the top down was one of my favorite things. The Cabriolet was white and roughly shaped like a marshmallow, so that's what I lovingly called her. She was slightly older but far better than any other car I'd ever driven. Because she was paid for, and she was mine.

A wolf whistle split the night air and drew my lips into a smile.

I turned to find Sheriff Wright headed my way, a bag of takeout in his grip.

"You know we don't go around whistling at one another around here," I told him, not for the first time. "It's sexist, rude and simply not done."

"I was just whistling," he said, a wide grin matching my own. "Takes some kind of self-importance to assume a whistling man is doing it for you."

I rolled my eyes and shut the passenger door, sealing Clyde and the carrier inside. "More takeout?" I asked, dragging my gaze from his pale-blue eyes, to the dusting of stubble over his cheeks, chin and jawline, before taking a minute to admire those perfect-for-whistling lips. "You really need to learn to cook."

Mason shrugged. "I don't have to. The women around here bring me casseroles faster than I can eat them. I thought I'd get a little pie tonight."

He gave the bag a gentle shake.

I bristled. "You know you could've stopped at Bless Her Heart and had a piece of my pie."

His grin widened, and I felt my cheeks flush.

"I have to go," I said. "Enjoy your…dessert."

"Now, wait a minute," he said, following me to the driver's side of my car. "I was on my way to see if you wanted to split this with me."

I looked from the bag to the man before me. "Why?"

He shrugged, trying a little too hard for nonchalance. "In case you wanted to talk about whatever I overheard this morning outside The Truck Stop."

I groaned. "I do not. That was nothing, and I've got it covered." I opened my door and dropped my purse behind my seat.

"Didn't sound like nothing," Mason said, folding his arms and widening his stance. "You looked pretty mad. So did Mr. Fryer."

"Nope."

"People are saying he threatened Clyde, then you threatened him," Mason said, voice deceptively cordial. "I only caught the end of the exchange, so I don't want to go on gossip alone. You sure you don't want to have some dessert and talk it over?"

"People should really mind their own business," I said sweetly, hoping he knew I included him in the statement. "Thank you for thinking of me to share your dessert, but everything is fine, and I've got an errand to run before I head home."

I got into the car and closed my door.

Mason watched me through the window as I buckled up and started the engine.

I waved before shifting carefully into gear and angling away from the curb.

Clyde rolled in his crate, catching me in his luminous gaze at the stop sign on the corner.

"That man makes me crazy," I told him. "He's everywhere, and he's nosy." I turned left and motored around the narrow end of the square, dividing my attention between The Truck Stop and Mason, who remained in the road where I'd left him.

He tracked me with his gaze in return.

"He's going to stand there and watch me take these carvings back to Fryer," I said, feathers beginning to ruffle.

The Truck Stop was dark as I made my next left turn and crept passed the window.

"Darn." I'd missed Mr. Fryer. Probably while I was talking to the nosy sheriff. "So much for putting this argument to rest tonight."

I made another two lefts, passing Mason and my shop a moment later.

He stared into my window as I rolled by.

I kept my eyes on the road, and made a right when I reached the next stop sign, heading away from downtown.

The bag of stolen carvings seemed to radiate energy from my purse, reminding me half the town probably thought I was a bully, based on the circulating gossip about my heated exchange with Mr. Fryer.

Worse, my mischievous cat had, in fact, taken some things that were important to Mr. Fryer. And perhaps the man's irritation with me was justified. Though, he really should've told me what was happening sooner, and directly, instead of leaving petty little notes where messages of gratitude should have been.

My blood pressure rose as I contemplated all the things that should've happened differently or not at all. And now I had to wait another day to get my apology over with.

The only thing I hated more than confrontation was waiting. Now I had to do both.

I pulled off the road and dialed Gigi. I had a new idea, which was a longshot, but worlds better than waiting another day to finish what had been started with Mr. Fryer.

"Hello, Bonnie," she answered brightly. "Did you forget something?"

"No." I sighed, checking my rearview mirror for signs Mason had followed me. "Any chance you know where Joe Fryer lives? The Truck Stop is already closed for the night, and I want to get my apology over with."

"Didn't he buy the house beside the woman who puts all her earthly possessions on the lawn every morning?" she asked.

"I'm not sure," I said. But I knew the place she meant. "I think that's some kind of ongoing estate sale. I bought the silver lamps on the bookcase there last month."

"Huh," she said. "I just thought she was, you know…" She let the sentence hang, and I imagined her circling one finger around her ear in the universal sign for cuckoo. "I guess I should stop and check out the sale sometime."

"You should," I agreed. "Do you know the address?"

I could picture the home with the big sale, but couldn't recall the street it was on. The home was enormous and must've been a mansion when it was built in the early twentieth century. I could barely picture the home at its side. A farmhouse, I thought.

The other homes on the street were built decades later and lined up like little soldiers in both directions, making the mansion and farmhouse stand out all the more.

"Hold on," Gigi said. "I'm texting Mirabelle. She knows everything."

Mirabelle was the local octogenarian crime reporter. She and Gigi were friends, mostly, and Gigi was right. Mirabelle knew everything.

"Yep," Gigi said. "The white farmhouse on Good Luck Lane. I didn't get a street number."

"No problem." I put my phone on speaker, typed in the street name, then set the device in the cup holder. "I'm all set. Thank you! And thank Mirabelle for me."

"Will do," she said. "Will we see you tomorrow for breakfast? Your father's making buckwheat pancakes."

"Maybe." According to the clock, it was already nearing eight, and I still had a lot of work to do at my new house on Cromwell Lake. "If I get to bed before midnight, I'll be there, but I don't know how long this thing with Mr. Fryer will take, and I want to paint my kitchen tonight."

Gigi groaned. "You young people work too much. I'm going home to watch my stories and get some sleep."

I said my goodbyes to Gigi and pointed Marshmallow in the direction of Good Luck Lane.

The double-wide gravel driveway came into view a few minutes later.

Clyde meowed, long and low, as I slowed to make the turn.

"Only one more stop," I promised him. "I'll do my best to make this quick, then we'll go home and have a nice warm dinner. Shredded chicken and carrots for you. And because I'm tired and lazy, probably the same thing for me."

I parked the car out front and stared at the dark house. Clearly this was going to be even quicker than I'd imagined. It didn't appear as if anyone was home. "I'll be right back," I told Clyde, then climbed into the night.

An old farm truck with bulbous fenders and THE

TRUCK STOP painted down the side was parked before the closed doors of a detached garage. I couldn't help wondering if that was by design, for maximum advertising, or if his garage was a workshop and there wasn't room to park inside.

He had to have somewhere to create all his designs, after all.

I fished the bag of carvings and my apology note out of my purse, then carried it to the door.

No one answered when I knocked, so I tried the bell, already wondering if it was acceptable to leave the bag on the knob.

A slow creaking sound caught my ear from alongside the home, and I leaned over the porch railing, peering into the darkness. "Hello?"

A soft shuffling sound lifted on the wind, but no one responded or answered the door.

Goosebumps rose on my arms as a cool night breeze picked up, and suddenly, a dozen grim memories skittered through my mind. Memories of dangerous nights and threatened loved ones. Memories I wished I didn't have, and ones I surely didn't want to add to.

I hung the bag on the doorknob, my simple apology note tucked inside. I could drop by The Truck Stop tomorrow to ask if he received the items, though I couldn't imagine how he could miss them, or that anyone else would happen upon them, on his porch, after dark, then take off with them. *They're safe enough*, I reasoned, and I wanted to be sure I was too.

With one last look at the home, I darted back to my car and zipped down the lane to the main road, eager to get home and triple lock my door.

CHAPTER FOUR

I woke alert and ready for work the next day. Mostly, so I could drop by The Truck Stop and make sure Mr. Fryer got my note and gift. I'd forgone plans to paint when I got home in favor of baking, the only thing that ever truly distracted my frantic mind.

So, I'd gotten straight out of bed with my alarm, prepped myself and Clyde for work, then discovered I had more than an hour to kill before it made any sense to head downtown.

Luckily, we lived on a lake now.

I carried my new Mr. Coffee down the single cement step to my rear patio and plugged him in on a table near the back door. Then I wrapped myself in a light blanket, lowered into a bright red Adirondack chair and pointed myself toward the waters.

This was my happy place. A large cement pad outside my rear door, overlooking Cromwell Lake. The patio had a stone firepit, a pair of small folding tables, my Adirondack chair and ottoman. Now, also me and Mr. Coffee.

The lake house was a near travesty when my real estate agent showed it to me a few months ago. Before I'd realized my snake of an ex was hiding actual millions from me, I'd put in the best bid I could manage, based on limited personal savings and the faith of our local bank. At the time, a travesty was all I could afford. But I didn't mind then or now because I was building a life out of making old things new again, myself included, and the view of Cromwell Lake from this backyard was priceless.

The lake house was a one-story cottage built in the early 1940s by a businessman in New Jersey who liked the idea of spending his summers on a lake more than he liked actually spending summers on a lake. He rarely used the place but enjoyed having the option, so the home sat empty for the better part of eighty years. When the original owner died, the property passed down the family line to others who had no interest in visiting or moving or selling a piece of family property. Until its most recent owner, who lived in the Pacific Northwest, saw the fiscal imprudence of paying property taxes for the rest of his life on a home he'd never seen and wouldn't visit. So, the lakefront cottage and its 1.87 acres of green grass and willow trees went on the market just when I wanted to buy.

I'd made mental notes about how to repair and update the place the moment I'd seen it, and my unexpected divorce-fueled windfall made those changes all the easier. The interior still had a ways to go, but I was hiring local and willing to be patient.

A demolition team removed most of the walls before new studs were brought in and erected. Then an electrician and plumber replaced all the pipes and wiring before new drywall was hung. The floors, which had been destroyed by animals that had found their ways inside over the years, were replaced with wide-planked, high-polished wood. A kitchen renewal team was working this week, attempting to preserve as much of the original cabinetry as possible while making room for larger, more modern appliances, and the rest was up to me. Paint. Décor. Furnishings. I had notebooks full of ways to make my modest 1,200 square feet feel like something straight out of a design catalogue, and I couldn't wait to see it through.

I inhaled the fresh morning air, tinged with bitter tendrils of steam from my coffee, and propped my feet on the pillow-topped foot stool before me.

This was the kind of peace everyone needed.

I set my head back, content with absolutely everything and gazed at the fog looming over the water.

The sound of tires on my driveway broke the silence and set me on my feet. If my folks had brought breakfast, I would call this day my best of the year.

My ringing doorbell echoed through the home's back screen door.

"I'm here!" I called cheerfully into the crisp morning air, enjoying my beautiful home and surrounding views. "On the patio."

The lake house's exterior was nearly perfect. I'd hired a man and his son to manage the lawn and keep the fields around my home too short for mice and snakes to enjoy. And having parents who owned and operated a flower farm came in handy more than ever before. They had a mulch guy who delivered in bulk with a big dump truck at no extra charge, and they'd brought flowers and shrubs by the pickup load.

Painters had scraped the old, chipping paint from the home's cedar shake before repainting the whole thing a serene shade of gray-blue and adding long, narrow shutters. Gigi had installed window boxes and filled them with the kinds of flowers that hung in curtains over the sides.

I'd never been happier with a purchase in my life.

Or with a place.

Quick footfalls padded along the walk to my patio.

"Please have pancakes. Please have pancakes," I chanted softly, twisting to get a look at my visitor.

"Bonnie?" Mason's voice called, scrambling my thoughts.

"Mason?"

He appeared a moment later, the usual frown in place. He hadn't brought breakfast or anything I could see. And so far all he'd said was my name.

"Good morning?" I asked, testing his mood.

He set his hands on his hips. "No."

"Coffee?" I motioned to Mr. Coffee on the table near the screen door. "I baked last night if you want something sweet to go with it."

"You baked?" he asked. "Was there something on your mind when you got home?"

I smiled, using a hand to shade the sun from my eyes. "Careful, it sounds as if you know me, Sheriff."

His lips pressed into a tight white line and made no move toward the coffee.

"What's wrong?" I asked, slightly irritated that he'd come to sour my mood.

Then another thought pressed the air from my lungs. I pulled my feet from the ottoman and tucked them beneath me. "Are my folks okay? Is Gigi? Is this one of those times local law enforcement comes to tell the family there was an accident?"

My throat clogged and my heart raced.

"Your family is fine," he said, "as far as I know anyhow. This isn't about them."

I sighed deeply in relief. "Then what's it about?"

"Joe Fryer."

"Oh, him."

Mason took a seat on the foot stool and rested his forearms on his thighs, bringing him impossibly close. "When was the last time you spoke with Mr. Fryer?"

The scent of Mason's cologne, shampoo and soap light-
ened my head. The combination was magnificent— intoxi-
cating. Uniquely, perfectly him. I wasn't sure if I'd rather eat
it or bathe in it. I imagined yanking him close and pressing
my nose against the skin of his throat then inhaling to the
point of collapse.

"Are you even listening to me?" he chided.

I snapped back to reality, chastising myself for the
bizarre, and poorly timed, fantasies I'd been experiencing
lately. I supposed it was from sleeping in a home full of
drywall dust, or maybe there was hallucinogenic mold
growing on the foundation. "What?"

"When did you last speak to Joe Fryer?" he repeated.

"Yesterday."

"And where were you last night?" he asked, his frown
giving way to the blank cop face I hated.

"Home."

I scrambled backward over my thoughts, seeking the
obviously important part of the conversation I'd missed, but
all I could recall was an image of me aggressively sniffing
Mason's Adam's apple, and my cheeks flushed.

His right eyebrow rose. "What aren't you telling me?"

"Nothing. I was here all night."

"Why didn't you want me to come over?" he challenged.

"I always want you to come over."

That earned me a second eyebrow and my cheeks grew
hotter.

"No," he said flatly. "You didn't. I bought us a dessert to
share, and you told me you didn't want it. You said you had
an errand to run."

I wrinkled my nose. He was right to be suspicious. I never
turned down dessert.

"Where did you go after work last night, besides home?"
he pressed.

My night rushed back to me, and I froze, realizing what must've happened. Fryer found my apology and bag of recovered carvings, and he called the cops. For what? Aggressive neighborliness? Unwanted apologies? "I stopped by Mr. Fryer's house," I admitted.

Mason scrubbed a hand over one side of his face and a healthy dose of stubble.

I'd spent my entire afternoon looking for those little carvings, then I'd driven them to his home. That wasn't enough? Was there any end to his crotchetiness?

"What did he say when he saw you?" Mason asked.

I frowned. "Nothing. He never saw me."

Mason groaned. "Bonnie. I need you to think before you answer."

My frown became a scowl. "Whatever he's saying is a lie. You know that, right?"

When Mason's eyes met mine, the expression was both stern and fearful. "He didn't say anything. The man's dead. The paperboy found his body on the front porch."

I blinked. "What?"

"All those people heard you fighting with him yesterday," Mason said quietly. He scooted to the edge of my ottoman, until his hands were mere inches from my knees. "People were already saying you threatened him."

"I didn't," I said. "Not really. Are you sure he's dead?"

Mason nodded. "If there's anything you need to tell me, now is the time."

I felt his words like a slap when they registered. "Seriously?"

He lifted his palms in peace. "Just doing my job."

"As sheriff," I said. "What about your job as my friend?" I examined him more closely, taking in his stupidly well-fitting T-shirt and jeans. "Why aren't you wearing a jacket? It's fifty-seven degrees."

"Oh, I don't know," he said smartly. "Maybe I knew how much trying to talk to you about this would raise my temperature."

"Funny," I said.

Mason stared.

"I returned all those carvings Clyde stole and hung them on his door. Here." I swiped my phone to life, then flipped to the photo of Clyde towering over a portion of the town square in miniature. "See."

Mason frowned. "We didn't find any carvings on the porch."

"They were in a bag," I said. "I hung it on the knob. Maybe he took it inside before he was killed."

Mason rubbed a hand over his forehead, not looking convinced. "I don't know about that, but there is a silver lining. At least you aren't the only suspect this time around," he said, reminding me of the way we'd first met, when he'd accused me of killing a little old lady for her ball gowns. "This time, the killer left a note."

"A note?" I asked, stilling to wait for the answer.

"Yeah. It's not much to go on, but I think the lab will be able to make something of it."

"Was the note on golden cardstock with a single word written in messy black ink?" I asked, praying silently to be wrong.

Mason's eyes narrowed and his head cocked. "How do you know that?"

I dropped my head against the slats of my chair with a thunk. So much for my perfect morning. "Because I wrote the note."

CHAPTER FIVE

I waited for Mason to drive away before making a run for my things. I packed up and headed downtown in a flash, driving slowly past The Truck Stop's dark windows before circling back to my side of the square and parking outside Bless Her Heart.

I slung my purse on one shoulder and grabbed Clyde's carrier, then made a beeline for the coffee shop next door. I was going to need significantly more caffeine to deal with the storm that was already brewing. Soon, the entire town would know Fryer was dead, and they'd be looking in my direction for answers. Mason was right, a lot of people had seen or heard us arguing yesterday, and the gossip had already begun on that matter.

The old expression *timing was everything* was true, and the timing of my decision to investigate the origin of those mean messages truly stunk.

I mentally kicked myself as I stopped at the back of a long line to the coffee counter. I had to turn this Fryer situation around before people heard about the note found at the crime scene. On the surface, the whole thing seemed poetic.

He left me hostile notes, we faced off, people thought I'd threatened him, and he turned up dead with a note from me.

The worst part of the already terrible situation was that Mason hadn't found the bag of carved figures. Their absence made my story seem fake and me sound like a fibber.

"So not good," I muttered, shuffling slowly forward with the line.

A blond woman in front of me turned to smile. "The line's long but worth it," she said. Her bright blue eyes twinkled with her words. She had thick, dark lashes, and high, round cheekbones to rival any storybook princess. She'd tucked flowers into the golden waves of her hair, and I suddenly wished I'd taken more time with my own rowdy locks. "Have you had this coffee before? Pecan praline is my favorite. I can barely get myself going for lesser coffee these days."

I smiled, enchanted by her enthusiasm and general golden glow. "I'm familiar with the coffee," I said, having spent untold hours in this shop as a child with my folks and Gigi, then with friends as a teen. "I'm Bonnie," I said. "I run the second-chance shop next door."

Her naturally round eyes widened. "You're Bonnie Balfour? The infamous local sleuth?"

"Uhm." I looked around to see who was listening and which one of the onlookers might've put her up to this.

No one paid any attention.

"I don't know about infamous," I said carefully.

She smiled at the carrier in my hand, having turned to face me as we waited. "This must be Clyde! The other half of your dynamic duo."

I gave her a closer look, certain I was being punked.

She wore a pale-green-and-cream dress with a muted checkered design and a bow that tied at her back. White socks folded down over her ankles rimmed in a ribbon of eyelet lace. Old-fashioned kitten heels finished the unusual, though oddly fashionable, ensemble. And she had a small hard-sided pet carrier in her arms.

"I didn't catch your name," I said.

"Oh, I am so rude." She gave a self-deprecating grin. "What would Mama think! I'm Louisa Eggers, and this is my best friend, Thelma." She pinched the little door on her carrier open, and a flappy feathered chicken poked its head out.

"Buh – gawk!"

The shop's patrons turned in our direction, going quiet in unison.

"Sorry!" Louisa called, closing the little door once more. "Thelma's normally a real delight, but she's cautious about cats. You understand."

I stared at her, then at the chicken she had in a pet crate at a coffee shop, and barked an unexpected laugh. "I suppose that makes perfect sense," I said, wiping tears from the corners of my eyes. Clyde was her chicken's natural predator and all. Then another thought occurred. "So, you're Thelma and Louisa?" I smiled, certain another round of laughter was on its way. "Like from the movie?"

Louisa shook her head vehemently. "That was Thelma and Louise. I'm Louisa. Copyright infringement issues and all."

"Right," I said, unsure again if she was joking. "And your last name is Eggers?" I smiled. "Any relation to Travis Eggers?"

"Yes! He's my uncle," she said. "I'm from Cromwell, and I travel back and forth to care for Uncle Travis."

I nodded in understanding. Her uncle had been injured during an attack at the Enchanted Gardens last summer. He'd been lucky then, given the killer who'd gone after him. And luckier still to have a niece willing to care for him. "How's he doing?"

"He's been doing well for a while," she admitted sheepishly. "I honestly just drive over to check on him for the coffee."

The admission dumbfounded me. Cromwell was the town next door, visible across the lake where I lived and our town's biggest rival in everything from high school football to Rotary Club fundraising. Generally Blissers didn't speak the C word or ever cross the line between towns. I'd assumed the same was true for Cromwellians.

She offered a small sad smile. "I'm from the bespoke community. We don't pay any never mind to the rivalries"

I frowned. "What's a bespoke community?"

"You might be more familiar with the term cottage core?"

I shook my head.

Her smile turned serene. "It's a cultural movement toward an idealized country lifestyle. We live together and trade our wares. Everyone has something to contribute, even if that's just two free hands and some time. We live and work as a team. Looking out for one another," Louisa explained.

I thought of my family and friends and didn't see a big difference, but maybe I was missing something.

"Next!" Dave called from the counter, motioning us forward. He smiled when we stepped up. "Bonnie and Louisa," he called over his shoulder.

His daughter, Daisy, waved.

"You both want your usual?" Dave asked.

"Yes, please," Thelma and I said in unison, earning a chuckle from Dave.

"When did the two of you become friends?" he asked, writing our names on our respective cups before passing them to Daisy.

"Just now, I think," Louisa said, beaming so brightly, I let go of the fact that she was dressed like a dollhouse figurine and lived in Cromwell. Plus, I liked her chicken, and their names.

We paid, then stepped aside to wait for our drinks.

I warmed to her further as she stretched a finger into the carrier to stroke Thelma's head.

"I'm going to miss this place," she said on a soft exhale.

"Won't you be back?" I realized a moment later that she'd likely heard Blissful Bean was closing. "The new owner of this space plans to serve the same coffee at her bakery. So, even after Dave retires, your favorite morning pick-me-up will be around."

"I'm actually getting back to my egg enterprise," Louisa said, eyes brightening. "Now that my uncle doesn't need me anymore, I can work on it full time."

I looked at Thelma, curiously. "You have an egg enterprise?" How many eggs could a single hen lay?

"I'm starting one," she said proudly. "I'm a Polish hen breeder and collect a lot of eggs. I figured it was time I turn those eggs into cash that can help me better care for the hens." She tapped her phone screen a few times, then turned it to face me. A pen filled with scratching, bushy-headed chickens filled the screen. "That's my nanny cam live feed," she said. "I like to keep an eye on things when I'm away."

"Huh," I said. If I wanted to keep an eye on Clyde, I'd have to fasten a camera to his collar.

"I'm going to use the eggs to make soufflés. I plan to open a stand near my cottage next year."

"Louisa," Daisy called, setting her drink on the counter. "Thank you!"

"And Bonnie."

I took my cup and waited my turn to stuff a tip into the jar when Louisa finished.

"It was nice meeting you," I said. "If you need any help

decorating your soufflé stand, let me know. I love to support my fellow female entrepreneurs."

She nodded, then took her leave.

I floated to Bless Her Heart on the whimsy of a twenty-something woman raising Polish hens and opening a soufflé stand with their eggs. I might even cross the invisible Cromwell boundary line to get a look at that for myself someday.

I freed Clyde behind the counter and stowed the carrier away so I wouldn't trip over it. Then I flipped on all the lights, booted up my register and selected a Christmas music playlist.

Today was a day for sewing. I gathered my kit and notes about the upscaling of several newly acquired dresses, then set to ripping their seams. I had faith that the rack of fancy gowns would fly off their hangers as soon as women realized they had a dozen holiday parties to attend and nothing to wear.

Sleighbells jingled against my front door as the first guests of the day arrived.

Mom, Dad and Gigi piled inside with wary smiles, fresh flowers and what looked like a casserole dish.

"We heard what happened," Mama said, setting the bouquet on my counter before coming at me with open arms. Her denim overalls hung loose on her petite frame, and she was next to nothing in my embrace. "How are you doing, baby girl?" she asked, pulling back to tuck my hair behind one ear.

She'd folded a floral handkerchief into a triangle and fixed it over the top of her pulled-back hair. A smattering of freckles darkened the skin over her nose and cheeks, brought out by time spent in the sun. Gigi, Mama and I never tanned. It was impossible for our nearly transparent skin, but freckles loved to make an appearance, then multiply rapidly upon exposure to a single UV ray.

After that we burned.

Gigi set the dish on my refreshments stand. "I made coffee cake. It's still warm, if you want some."

"I'll make coffee," Dad said.

I raised my cup from Blissful Bean, then smiled at my beloved busybody family. "Thank you."

Dad still made coffee.

Gigi plated four slices of coffee cake, then ferried a slice to each of us. "We can't believe this is happening to you again," she said. "We were sure your luck had turned around."

I grimaced. Bliss's obsession with luck was profound. And often treated as if it was contagious. Anyone deemed as lucky, for example, would find themselves surrounded by friends ready to celebrate that good fortune and hoping a little would rub off while they were there. On the flip side, someone others viewed as unlucky could expect to be avoided like the plague.

I couldn't afford to be a plague. I had a business to run and an employee to pay. Not to mention, my business was useful to folks. My work mattered.

"Eat," Gigi said, passing me a fork for the coffee cake.

The warmth of the breakfast treat seeped through the thin paper plate, heating my hand.

Dad offered Mom and Gigi some coffee, then rested his back side against the counter and evaluated me. "What the heck happened at Fryer's place last night?"

"I don't know," I said. "No one was home when I got there."

He stroked his closely trimmed beard and locked me in a fatherly gaze. "Your mama and I were talking," he said.

I shoved a bit of breakfast between my lips to keep myself from arguing with whatever came next.

"We think you should stay with us until this whole thing blows over. We don't want to take a chance on you getting hurt again."

Mama moved to his side and his arm lifted, curling around her as she arrived. As if they were two parts of one whole being reunited.

I forced my attention back to the plate in my hand. I'd always wanted what they had, but I'd chosen very poorly, and that was it. I'd blown it.

I swallowed the bite of coffee cake and forced a confident smile. "I don't think we need to worry just yet. I spoke with Mason this morning, and he knows I wouldn't do this."

Mama frowned, and deep worry lines appeared on her forehead. "It must be so hard on him to be put in this position all the time." She set a palm on Dad's middle. "It would kill me to investigate Bud for a crime I knew he didn't commit. It would be the same for him, I'm sure."

Dad nodded.

"Well, I'm not being investigated," I said, feeling my feathers ruffle. "And Mason isn't my husband of forty-plus years, so there are some big differences in your comparison." I stuffed another bite of coffee cake between my lips.

My family looked at me as if I was a puppy at a pound.

"Mason and I are friends," I said, shoveling in another hunk to follow the last.

The sweet cinnamon topping melted on my tongue, and my eyes shut.

"He has to follow the evidence," Dad said. "Which makes you the main suspect."

"Again," Mama added.

I swallowed, then huffed. "A few people heard us arguing yesterday. Yes. But people fight. It doesn't mean they kill each other."

I thought of my apology note found at the crime scene

and decided to keep that tidbit to myself. Otherwise, Dad might attempt to bodily remove me from the shop and lock me in my childhood bedroom for safe keeping.

Mama tipped her head to rest on his arm. "I'm sure you're right. But the offer to stay with us stands. Our door is always open."

"I know." I stepped forward and kissed her cheek, then Dad's. "I'm going to be just fine."

Gigi made a face that suggested she thought I was nuts.

"Stop it," I told her. "No one knows I was at Fryer's place last night, except you guys and Mason." Clearly Gigi had shared that information with my parents over breakfast.

"And Mirabelle," Gigi said.

My jaw dropped, and I bumbled to the closest armchair. Mirabelle had given Gigi the address for me.

And as the town's only crime reporter, she'd surely been at the scene today.

I made a choking sound.

This really was bad luck.

CHAPTER SIX

I spent the next two hours finishing the adjustments on a red velvet dress with black buttons and a matching red crinoline, then I moved on to flower arranging.

I filtered the fresh flowers Mama had brought me this morning into already full vases on my counter, removing droopy and browning petals and buds as I worked. I'd added thick bands of ribbon on the larger vases to match the fall décor and set an assortment of gourds and pumpkins at their bases, near a series of potted succulents that had been gifted to me by a friend.

Gigi kicked back in a tufted armchair, her little feet propped on an oversized hassock, reviewing her plans for the bakery. She'd brought paperwork on everything from local advertising and marketing opportunities to notebooks with public-relations ideas.

She was giving the bakery launch much more logical thought than I had when I decided to lease the space for Bless Her Heart. I'd been emotional and desperate for a new start, running on fumes and the *if I build it, they will come* mentality. It had taken an enormous amount of time and perseverance after opening the doors just to get folks to come inside.

Gigi wouldn't have that problem. She was making a plan.

I turned my attention to the distant shop across the square. I couldn't seem to stop staring at The Truck Stop's window, recalling the petty and unproductive argument I'd incited by showing up there yesterday. And thinking about how different things could've been if I'd listened to Lexi, the teenage voice of reason.

I gave the rearranged bouquet a final fluff, then stepped around my counter, still staring across the way. It was difficult to be sure from this distance, but The Truck Stop seemed to be open. Was that possible?

Did Fryer have a business partner? Did his employees not know he was dead? Did he even have any employees?

If my body had been found a handful of hours ago, I wouldn't want my shop open for business as usual. Would he?

"So far, so good," Gigi said, abandoning her comfy chair and sneaking up behind me. "I just checked the Get Blissed Facebook page and no one's posted about you or Fryer yet today. You can go do your thing without too much hassle, I think."

"What's Get Blissed?" I asked, also wondering what exactly she thought I could now go and do.

Gigi frowned and fluttered a hand between us. "You remember. The Facebook group Cami set up for shops and locals to share news and events. It turned into a big old gossip fest," she said, raising her phone into view, a wicked gleam in her eye. "It's shameless."

I moved around the counter to her side and squinted at the screen. I wasn't sure I remembered the thing she was talking about, and I could barely read the screen. "Can you make this bigger?"

Gigi pumped up the font size. "You should get your eyes checked."

"I have perfect vision. I always have."

She shrugged. "You're nearly forty. You might need glasses."

"I don't need glasses." I moved closer to the screen, trying to remember having seen the group before. Now that I was looking, it was a little familiar.

"Our bodies change," she pressed on. "Our eyes get weaker, tired and wonky shaped, kind of like the rest of us."

I frowned. "My eyeballs aren't wonky shaped." Hopefully neither was the rest of me. "Is it a private group?" I asked, hoping to change the subject.

"It is now," she said. "Cami made it a secret group when it got out of control like this. Now, you have to ask to be added. She set up a page for announcing news and events, where only she can post."

"Live and learn," I said.

Gigi giggled. "That's the truth. We have to let her know if there's something we want announced."

"So this is just a gossip group now?"

"Pretty much," she said. "You have to request to join, prove you live here and promise to keep it clean." She chuckled. "No one listens."

"Weird."

"And fun," Gigi said. "I get notifications on new posts, and I plan to use this group like a police scanner to keep my finger on the pulse of local gossip mill until your name is cleared."

"I'm not under investigation," I said. "Mason knows I didn't hurt Mr. Fryer."

"But you did leave an apology note with his corpse."

I imagined poking her. "I left it in a bag on the doorknob. His corpse was nowhere to be seen."

"Still, things aren't looking great for you," she said.

"That's only because all the evidence leads to me right now."

Gigi tented her brows, as if to say, *Oh, much better.*

"I'll just have to make sure Mason gets more and better evidence," I said.

"And how do you plan to do that?"

I raised my eyes to the window overlooking the square and clocked a small figure in the distance, moving back and forth in front of The Truck Stop.

"Do you see that?" I asked, moving to stand in front of my glass shop door. "I think someone is posting something on Fryer's window."

"Who?" Gigi asked. "What?"

A jolt of adrenaline raised me onto my toes. I spun back to her with renewed enthusiasm and purpose. "Gigi?"

"I'll hold down the shop," she said. "But be careful, and bring me a pastrami sandwich on your way back, would ya? I can't survive on coffee cake alone."

"Done!" I made a mental note about the sandwich and darted outside.

I took my time crossing the square, keeping watch on my surroundings, specifically for signs of Mason, who would deeply disapprove of my going anywhere near Mr. Fryer's shop today.

And I hurried ahead.

A cluster of shoppers stood a respectful distance away from The Truck Stop, whispering as they read the sign affixed to the window. A broad black banner with a pickup truck outlined in white drove along the tops of three words.

CLOSED FOR GRIEVING

I kept my eyes down as I made my way up the front step to knock.

A woman peered through the door's window, then pointed to the sign.

I waved.

The door sucked open, and she glared with red-rimmed eyes. "We are closed. There was a death in the family."

"I'm Bonnie Balfour," I said. "I run the shop across the square. May I please come in?"

Behind me, a murmur of whispering voices grew.

The woman lifted her gaze over my shoulder, and I knew from experience she could only see half of my shop from here, thanks to a whole mess of leafy oak trees on the square.

I did my best to appear as sullen as possible when she returned her gaze to mine.

"Fine. Come in."

I stepped over the threshold and waited while she locked up behind me.

"I'm Jean," she said, crossing her arms and towering over me. Her voice was husky, like a blues singer's, but raspy, as if the singer smoked two packs a day.

I was five-foot-two, and I guessed Jean at five-foot-ten or more.

I took a step back.

Her long salt-and-pepper hair was unkempt and wiry. Her fitted black T-shirt and jeans emphasized a generous figure and displayed an abundance of wrinkled cleavage at my precise eye level that I would never unsee.

I cleared my throat and squared my shoulders, struggling to put my head back in the game. "I was very sorry to hear about…" I motioned to the sign on the window, unsure how to proceed. Eventually, I landed on, "Your loss."

She grunted.

I considered the sound. Was Fryer's death a loss to her?

Who was she? And why was she here?

"Did you know him well?" she asked. "Or are you one of those women who try to interject yourself into trauma situations for the attention?"

"Neither." I performed a quick self-check to confirm my answer. Definitely neither.

She dragged her gaze over my sensible cotton dress and matching flats, then shook her head, clearly unimpressed. "Look at all those people gathering like buzzards."

I frowned, feeling uncomfortably like Queen of the Buzzards, considering I was the only one pushy enough to come to the door. "I saw the sign," I said in explanation for my boldness. "This store's been here a while, but I just met the owner yesterday. Today, he's gone. It's hard to get my head around."

"Well, Hotrod was old," she said. "Maybe he had a stroke or something. I heard the paperboy found him."

"I'm not sure," I said, knowing that if it was anything other than murder, Mason wouldn't have graced me with his grumpy presence this morning. There hadn't been enough time for an autopsy before his visit, but the coroner usually had a good idea of what he was dealing with after an initial evaluation at the scene of death.

My mind halted and took three big steps backward. "Did you call Mr. Fryer *Hotrod*?" I tried to imagine the curmudgeonly old man as anything other than that and failed.

"Did you just call Hotrod *Mr. Fryer*?"

She laughed. "Hotrod was his club name. I don't have a club name. Guys only."

I frowned. "You know Mr. Fryer through a club you don't belong to?"

Did I dare ask what sort of guys' club?

"The Road Crew," she said. "It's a truck club for historic pickup owners." She motioned to the shop's contents and all the many variations of old farm trucks around us. "We love classic pickups. We meet at the Crossroads Diner on Route Forty-two a couple nights a week to show off, share a meal and talk shop. It's mostly retired men, but they let a few ladies hang around. It's a lot of fun. We get plenty of support honks as folks drive by, and a lot of compliments from connoisseurs who come for dinner and walk the lot."

"You have an old pickup?" I asked, working on small talk while I mentally sorted the new information.

The note I'd seen near Fryer's phone yesterday had the words *road crew* on it. And that was apparently referring to his old-man truck club?

Strangely, it made more sense than Mr. Fryer meeting with a literal road crew.

"Nah," Jean said, answering the question I'd nearly forgotten I'd asked. "No truck for me. I'm more of a super-fan." She bobbed her head in agreement with herself and sighed. "A groupie."

I forced a tight smile, determined not to unpack all the things I didn't like about women being called groupies, or hanging out with men who didn't allow them to be directly associated. "Were you with the Road Crew last night?" I asked. "Was Mr. Fryer?"

"Sure. He never missed a meeting. I never miss a meeting either, but I'm usually the last to arrive. That'll always be the case since there's no way I'll ever afford to retire on my salary."

"And he seemed okay when you saw him?" I asked.

"Same as always," she said.

"When did he leave?"

She paused to think before answering. "Probably around six-thirty," she said. "He wanted to head home before it got too dark. Trouble driving at night maybe. Happens to the best of us."

I concentrated on the mental math, which added up. I'd arrived at Mr. Fryer's home around 7:30. Not exactly, but not much later. I wasn't sure how long it took to get from Crossroads Diner to Fryer's home, but it seemed possible for him to have easily made the trip before my arrival. Which would explain the truck outside his garage. Had he been inside with his killer when I'd arrived?

A shiver skittered down my spine and rattled me from head to toe.

Jean seemed to notice. Her disposition turned guarded and careful, as it had been when I'd first arrived. "Why are you asking about Hotrod like this?"

"Curiosity," I said. "It's my worst trait. How did you get a key to this place?" I asked, in a true example of my affliction.

"Key code," she corrected. "Hotrod gave me the code to his keyless entry a few months ago when I came to help one weekend. I thought I'd stop by today and do something nice for him. Let folks know he was gone."

Jean and I locked gazes as I began to wonder what kind of person would let themselves into a dead guy's place of business and hang a sign announcing his death, only to call the sign readers *buzzards*.

Something like recognition suddenly flared in Jean's narrowed eyes, and her gaze flicked quickly to the window. "Which shop across the street did you say was yours?"

I reached behind me to grip the doorknob and twisted the little lock to set me free. "I should let you get back to what you were doing."

"Bonnie," she said, a little breathy, as if my name suddenly meant something more to her. "You're the one with the cat!"

I pushed the door open and stumbled onto the step. "I don't think so. Thank you for your time. Condolences," I added, rushing onto the sidewalk before I made her angry. I had enough eyes on me already.

CHAPTER SEVEN

I hurried past the group of onlookers on the sidewalk, heading for Gigi's favorite sandwich shop, Pita Pan. She was addicted to their pastrami sandwich with all the traditional Italian sub ingredients and condiments. I preferred their chicken pesto, but if I was being honest, I'd eat anything from Pita Pan. The ingredients were always fresh and the pitas soft and warm. The scents alone nearly lifted me off my feet as I entered and placed my order.

The interior was long and narrow. Green tables and chairs. A white service counter. Most folks took their pitas to go, but a couple was snuggling and kissing in the corner as I handed the cashier my loyalty card. Thanks to Gigi's love of pastrami, I was working double time toward a free pita and chips.

I thanked the woman at the service counter and stepped away with my receipt, then marched toward the kissing couple with a smile. "Cough," I said. "Cough. Cough."

Cami pulled back from her new boyfriend and blushed, as she should. "Bonnie," she said, breathlessly. "What are you doing here?"

"Ordering lunch," I said. "And watching the show."

Her boyfriend, Dale, Mason's FBI pal, had the decency to look embarrassed. He offered me a hand to shake. "It's good to see you again. How are things?"

"Clearly not as good as your things," I teased. "But okay."

He nodded, and Cami reapplied her lipstick with a shaky hand and small compact.

"We got carried away," she said, sounding slightly more like herself. "Do you think anyone else saw us?"

"Making out in a public corner?" I looked around the otherwise empty dining area. "I don't know, but it's good to see the honeymoon phase hasn't faded."

Cami and Dale weren't married, but they'd fallen in love at first sight several months ago, as Gretchen at Golden Matches had predicted. And despite the fact that Dale lived in Ohio, they were frequently attached at the hip.

Dale traveled back and forth from Ohio to Georgia regularly now, and rumor had it he was considering a more permanent arrangement. Since he could do his job from anywhere, I was inclined to think he just might.

"Sit," Dale said. "Visit."

Dale was bulky and muscled where Mason was lean and lithe. He had brown skin and eyes with a face made for billboards. Together, he and Cami looked like an ad for beautiful people.

I took the seat across from Cami and grinned. "It's nice to see you forget yourself from time to time," I said.

Camilla Rose Swartz was runway-model fresh at all times, and had been since we'd met while feeding ducks on the lake in preschool. She'd been five inches taller than me since puberty and blessed with dewy, flawless brown skin all her life. She was kind to the core and no nonsense in the extreme. She was the one I called when I needed to move a mountain. She was my person.

Cami rolled her eyes. "I think the pressure to make this unique and outstanding village of ours into a budding tourist destination has gotten to me. I haven't kissed in public since high school."

Dale beamed proudly at this. Apparently honored to be the man who caused Cami to lose her wits.

"Which reminds me," Cami went on. "Are you participating in the Makers Market Friday?"

"Of course."

Cami had been operating a town-wide weekly event she called the Makers Market for months, advertising in the weekly *Bliss Bugle*, via flyers and by continuous word of mouth. The idea was to get all the locals who created, made or otherwise produced a tangible, salable item in one place at one time. It brought added exposure to small business owners, crafters and artisans, while helping those same people to network and make connections with buyers and other businesses. Some had even joined efforts, like home-made dog-treat bakers offering a coupon to use at the groomer, or buy something from the local jewelry maker and get a fancy hair accessory from the booth next door at a discount.

"I'm setting up a sidewalk sale," I told her. I planned to sell redesigned holiday décor, heavy on the Thanksgiving theme with a dash of items for Christmas.

"Perfect." She dropped her signature red lipstick back into her bag with a smile.

Dale winked, his deep-set brown eyes still gleaming, and clasped Cami's hand on the table when she'd put her makeup away. "Have you spoken to Mason about that thing yet?"

My eyelids fell briefly shut. I reopened them with a moan. That *thing* was the fact that Dale had told me about Mason's ex-girlfriend, Ava, while Dale and I worked together to find the money my ex had hidden. Dale had been worried about

Mason's well-being and confided his recent trauma. A story that probably wasn't his to tell and certainly not mine to know. But for a deeply concerned friend, a thousand miles away, it had seemed worth the risk to lay it out there. So someone in Mason's current life and world could keep an eye on him and make sure he was okay.

I'd been carrying the secret, with incredible guilt for knowing it, since then. And I needed to tell him I knew. Otherwise, I was tainting and potentially damaging our friendship, and I really liked our friendship.

I hung my head in continued shame.

Dale frowned at me.

Cami made sad puppy eyes. "We heard about Mr. Fryer," she said, changing the subject to something only slightly less complicated. "You argued with him yesterday and now he's gone. You must feel awful."

"I do."

Dale tented his thick black brows. "You must look guilty."

"I do."

Cami elbowed his ribs.

"What?" he asked. "Fighting publicly with someone who turns up dead is not a good look. I'll bet that's making Mason nuts."

"You have no idea," I said. Then I took a minute to fill them in on everything I knew so far.

They traded a long, horrified look.

Dale sipped from his drink on the table. "Yep. Mason is definitely flipping his lid."

"He is," I assured. "And I was just trying to do something nice. Now I'm dragged into another murder investigation."

The couple stilled, and I checked over my shoulder, worried Mason or a group of gossips had walked in.

The restaurant was still relatively empty, as were the sidewalks outside.

"Bonnie," Cami said slowly. "You aren't involved in a murder investigation. You aren't a real suspect, and there's no reason to get embroiled in this. Every time you travel this path, you get threatened and become endangered. Sometimes you get hurt."

"Not this time," I said. "This time I've only spoken to you two, plus Gigi and my folks." I thought of who else might know what I'd been up to, even if I hadn't discussed the details. Lexi for sure, and probably Mirabelle. "Oh, and I spoke to Jean over at The Truck Stop."

Dale snorted. "You mean the shop where the dead guy worked? The one surrounded by lookie-loos and gossip-mongers?"

"I was very discreet."

Cami's expression turned to genuine concern.

"I'm fine," I said. "Everything is good. Promise. You have absolutely zero reason to worry. Go back to kissing."

Dale's gaze swung toward the counter. The woman who'd taken my order was headed our way with a white logoed bag and a smile. "One Captain Hook, hold the pickle, and a Wendy with the works?"

"That's me," I said, accepting the bag and quickly pushing onto my feet. I waved my goodbyes to Dale and Cami, who appeared significantly less randy following our chat.

I made a mental note to take them a bottle of wine and an apology fruit basket one night very soon. They'd been having a good time before I showed up.

I crossed the street to Bless Her Heart, eager to dig into my pita and deliver Gigi's order before she got tired of waiting and ordered by phone.

My shop window and door décor were the definitions of perfection as I approached. An old rocking chair sat beside the table with my large red wrapped box and golden ribbon. Potted mums in crimson, gold and purple were positioned on a brown braided rug at the rocker's feet. Twinkle lights trimmed the window and doorframe. And beyond the window, dozens of oversized golden tags danced on red ribbons, each carrying words of gratitude from one Blisser to another.

I'd arranged a comfy chair, pillow, blanket and table before a small black fireplace unit. The layered, harvest-themed colors included a little pine green on the mantel and a basket with rolls of wrapping paper in gold, silver, white and crimson at the hearth. All coordinated to celebrate fall, with hints of Christmas to come.

Clyde dozed on the rug beneath a decorative table, one small crocheted turkey near his head. Stolen from the bookshelf near my dressing rooms.

I passed the carry-out bag to my left hand, freeing my right hand to lift the lid on my Gifts of Gratitude box and collect the slips inside.

My mind wandered back over the conversation with Jean, and I wondered how difficult it would be to borrow my dad's old farm truck. And if it would be so bad for me to make a trip to Crossroads Diner for dinner tomorrow. Perhaps run into Fryer's Road Crew while I was there. Maybe ask a question or two before Jean arrived.

Maybe Gigi would want to come with me as a lookout. We wouldn't be in any danger at a public place like Crossroads.

I flipped through the slips as I entered the shop, shamefully thankful to know there wouldn't be a single mean note waiting for me this time.

"Yes," Gigi called. "Pitas!"

I passed her the bag.

"What's in the box today?" she asked, arranging plates and napkins picnic-style on the counter.

"Gratitude for a local teacher," I said, warming at the kind words. "Praises for a long-time neighbor, celebration of a friend…"

My heart stopped and my mind scrambled as I stared at the final slip in my hand.

"What's wrong?" Gigi asked. "What does it say?"

I set the offending paper on the counter and accessed my cell phone to take a picture. I texted the image to Mason.

Fryer was dead, and I had a new stalker.

WATCH YOUR STEP BALFOUR

CHAPTER EIGHT

I stood in the living room that night, covered in sweat and steeped in frustration.

Mason had shown up at Bless Her Heart long enough to take my threat note, ask a bevy of pointed questions, then leave when his phone dinged. I'd spent the rest of my workday frustrated by his abrupt departure and anticipating his return.

He did not return.

So, Clyde and I came home to eat our feelings and take out our jazzed-up energies on the house.

I painted the entire place in varying shades of creamy vanilla, palest gray and good old-fashioned white. The idea of going so basic on every wall seemed incredibly unlike me on the surface, because I was a huge fan of color, but that wasn't what I wanted here. I wanted a clean canvas for my new home, something reflective of my new life. A palette I could enhance with subtle warmth added through accents, light fixtures, furnishings and décor. A peaceful backdrop to showcase the added pops of vibrancy.

A gentle breeze wafted through the open windows,

keeping me from getting too goofy off the paint fumes. I'd dressed the windows in custom curtains, hand stitched by me. I'd spent hours in fabric stores selecting exactly the right materials for each room, then matching those to my vision boards for the home and sewing them into existence at night, after long days at the shop and plenty of after-dinner baking.

I'd chosen sheer panels in a soft toile print for my front windows and used generous amounts of fabric, allowing the length to pool on the floor. The wispy material billowed and fluttered on the breeze, making me both happy and quite proud. I'd spent weekends with Mama and Gigi, traveling to flea markets and looking for all the right accents for every room. Until I'd purchased the lake house, I'd forgotten how much I enjoyed sewing for purposes other than mending.

Clyde stood guard at the glass storm door, peering at things he'd like to chase, steal or eat.

The sky beyond the glass was an enormous purple bruise, punctured by thousands of visible stars. Neighboring houses were just far enough away to give an illusion of isolation, and the lack of streetlights drove the illusion home.

I wiped a paint-spattered forearm across my brow and shuffled to the refrigerator, exhausted and deeply satisfied by my work. Also, I was starving. I'd stupidly let the new threat left inside my Gifts of Gratitude box spoil my lunch, and I'd begun painting before deciding what would be for dinner. Now I was too tired to cook and all I had was bottles of water and a lot of ingredients that looked less than appetizing on their own.

"Ugh," I grumped, collapsing dramatically onto a stool in the kitchen. I longed to flop forward onto the island with flair, but my countertops weren't going in until tomorrow.

I didn't have the energy to shower and redress just so I could pick up carryout, and ordering delivery would still mean facing the person bringing my food. So, I had a decision to make. Shower, clean up and place an order or suck it up and cook.

I dragged myself to the living room and sat on the floor, desperate not to get paint on my new furniture, and thankful I'd chosen hard woods instead of carpet. Wood would be easier to clean up.

My laptop looked back at me from the coffee table, and I dragged it closer, rethinking the delivery option. I could always hide behind the door when my meal arrived.

Instead, I found myself searching for the Facebook page Gigi mentioned earlier. When nothing in that feed caught my interest, I searched for the Road Crew.

Images of gray-haired men and a few women, wives or groupies, I presumed, appeared by the dozens. Along with a number of classic truck photos. I scanned every face for Mr. Fryer then every comment for his name.

I didn't find Fryer, but Jean appeared in multiple shots, hair teased to within an inch of its life and makeup applied by the pound. She was barely recognizable as the woman at The Truck Stop today. In the photos, she kind of looked like a groupie, just like she described herself, hanging on the men and posed on truck beds, soaking up attention.

Who knew that was a thing?

I clicked away from the photos and scrolled through the messages. It didn't take long to find someone named Hotrod exchanging heated words about a truck that had changed hands within the group. Hotrod had apparently purchased a 1953 Ford F100 pickup from a club member named Axel. He'd paid roughly ten thousand dollars, but according to the comments, the price was a significant undercut, and Axel called Hotrod a lowballer. With no other takers on the table, he was forced to accept the offer, and the discussion quickly devolved. Moderators shut the commenting down.

I wrinkled my nose. A deal was a deal, but taking advantage of a friend was dirty.

"Knock knock," Mason called through the glass storm door, a blessed bag of takeout in hand.

I could have kissed him.

Clyde swept back and forth against the glass at the sight of him, attempting to welcome and pet our guest.

I deeply regretted going online before showering.

Mason mouthed the word *wow* and watched with unbridled delight as I pushed sweaty, paint-smudged hair away from my cheeks and eyes.

"Shut up," I said, unlocking the door. "I've been painting. Now, come on in. Try not to bring the bugs."

Clyde chattered and pranced, nose and tail in the air as he followed a moth to my kitchen light. The moth paid the cat no mind. So, Clyde resolved to sit beneath the fixture and cry.

I understood the sentiment. I also hated bugs.

"You're a mess," Mason said, turning in a slow circle to absorb the half-finished home around him. "And this looks both worse and better than the last time I was here. Cleaner and more updated, but with less normal house parts."

"What's in the bag?" I asked, feeling drool form on my tongue.

"Loaded baked potatoes and chicken noodle soups."

"Bless," I said, exhaling the word. "Have a seat. I'll get the drinks. Is water okay?"

Mason nodded, eyes still scanning the partially finished space. "Water's fine, but where's the rest of your house?"

"This is it," I said, returning with two bottles from the fridge. I took a seat on the floor beside the couch.

"But where are the walls?" Mason asked, opening the take-out bag to divvy up the contents. "Where are your countertops?"

"Walls are gone," I said, digging greedily into my giant potato. Bacon bits and cheese fell off in piles as I lifted the first bite to my mouth. "It's open concept. I wanted to be able to see everyone when I had company. Cabinets will be installed Friday. The bedrooms, bath and mud room are back there." I pointed to the wall along the back of the kitchen, indicating the space on the other side. "Laundry is in the mud room with a back door to the patio. Oh my glory, this is heaven."

Mason frowned. "I'm going to need a tour. I liked the walls."

"I just finished painting," I said, chewing rudely as I spoke, too famished to stop eating just to talk. "It took twelve gallons. The new drywall just soaked up the coats."

Mason followed my gaze to the pile of empty paint cans on a drop cloth near the front door. Then he looked at my walls. "It's all white."

"It's not," I said, cracking the lid on my soup. "It's tranquil, and it's going to be fabulous." I inhaled the rich, mouthwatering steam as it rose from the cup, then gobbled the soup half down too.

Mason worked slowly through his meal, watching me more often than what he was doing. "I don't think I've ever seen you like this. Are you okay?"

"I'm fine." I packed my empty containers back into the bag and wished I could pop the button on my jeans. "I'm tired, and I feel a little frantic," I admitted. "I thought it was because I was hungry, but now I'm stuffed, and I still feel like someone threw a Mentos in my soda."

"And you are the soda?" he asked.

"Yeah."

"The note you received this afternoon probably didn't help," he said. "Any ideas about who might've left it?"

I shook my head. "Not really. Not yet."

Mason clucked his tongue and shook one long finger at me. "See. I don't like it when you use that word."

"Not?"

"Yet," he corrected. "It's a naughty word when you use it."

I grinned. "A naughty word."

"Yes." He nodded emphatically. "It means you are up to something. And that is never good."

I looked at his handsome, confident face, then at the meal I'd devoured like there might be a gold medal for speed and enthusiasm. "You talked to Dale, didn't you?"

And Dale had tattled on me. Possibly out of concern, but more likely because Cami was concerned, but he'd tattled nonetheless.

"No," Mason said, wiping a paper napkin across his lips. "I spoke to Jean at The Truck Stop. Why? What does Dale know?"

I bit my lip. "Nothing."

"Uh uh. No way, Balfour," he said. "Start talking or I'll call Dale and put him on speaker phone."

I frowned at his smug face. "Fine. He was with Cami at Pita Pan when I got lunch for me and Gigi."

"Was that before or after you pushed your way inside Mr. Fryer's store and questioned his friend?" Mason asked, taking another bite from his potato.

My jaw dropped. "Jean is a self-proclaimed groupie for his classic truck club, and told me she let herself into his shop today using the keycode he entrusted her with. She hung up a sign to let people know about his passing, then scoffed at everyone who took notice and read it. Who does that? Did you talk to her? What did she say?"

Mason wrinkled his nose. "She thought you were a mite suspicious. Her words, not mine. Personally, I find you extremely suspicious."

"She's the problem," I said, ignoring his jibe. "Not me.

Her." I turned my laptop to face him and waved a hand at the screen. "Look at this."

"Uh huh," Mason said, keeping his eyes on my screen, scrolling through the page contents. "So, you spoke to her about her relationship to the victim, learned about the classic truck club, then came home and looked them up?"

I stilled.

Mason turned his cool blue gaze on me, brows tented, waiting.

I looked away, fascinated by the paint on my pantleg.

"You're meddling in this investigation," he said. "And I think that might be the actual definition of nuts after all you've been through during your similar quests."

I shifted on the hard floor, hating my sore joints and numbing backside. "I have to get up before something I need falls asleep permanently," I said, pushing myself upright with the help of the couch. I rolled my neck and arched my back, feeling ten years older than I had when I woke this morning. "I'm not meddling."

"You really, really are."

I turned to face him, prepared to defend myself, when something came to mind. "Jean could've put that note in the gratitude box." The moment I spoke the words, I knew they were true. "She had plenty of time to deliver that note after we spoke, because I went to get lunch, and I talked with Dale and Cami at Pita Pan while I waited for my order," I said. "And she had no reason to be at The Truck Stop. She was basically trespassing. She could be the killer."

Mason watched me. "That would be your word against hers, but let's run with this. Why would she kill Joe Fryer?"

"I don't know," I said, pacing a small circle through the room. "Maybe she wanted to be his girlfriend, but he only wanted a groupie or help at the shop from time to time."

I deflated back to the floor, certain I'd just have to sleep there tonight because I'd never be able to get up again.

"Is that your final answer?" Mason asked. "No more suspects on the list you shouldn't have?"

"It could be Axel."

Mason blinked. "Who?"

"Axel." I moved in close, then took a seat at his side, hoping the paint on my pants was all dry by now. "May I?" I slid the laptop onto my knees and scrolled to the set of messages that had been shut down by the group's moderator. "Him." I tapped the screen with one finger. "I need a shower, but you can wait for me. Read this while I scrub the paint off my skin and change my clothes. When I come back, we'll have dessert."

Mason winked, and I hurried away, planning to make my shower a cold one.

CHAPTER NINE

The next day crawled by as I waited for Gigi to arrive at Bless Her Heart. She'd agreed to join me for dinner at the Crossroads diner, but she also had meal plans with my folks that she couldn't break without drawing suspicions. So, I watched the clock obsessively and sent up a silent prayer that she could persuade Dad to let us borrow the old farm truck for a made-up errand.

Gigi planned to say we needed the truck to pick up some patio furniture for the lake house. I needed patio furniture, so that worked out well, and as long as we bought some pieces tonight, I wouldn't be lying.

I hated lying.

Gigi had been pushing me to get a full matching set of wicker pieces for weeks, and I suspected this was her genius way of killing two birds with one stone.

I perused my shop, looking for additional ways to decorate without crossing the line between gorgeous and gaudy.

Clyde licked his sleek black fur as I approached, then rolled onto his back beneath some ball gowns. He stretched his paws overhead until he seemed twice his natural length, and I melted a little at his cuteness.

I stopped to snap a picture to share with anyone who'd look, then tucked the phone away.

The bells over my door jingled, and I turned toward the sound, hoping it was Gigi. "Welcome to Bless Her Heart."

Mirabelle marched inside, wearing a trademark tracksuit and dragging her old, overweight Pekingese, Mr. Dinky, by his leash. "Good. You're open," she said. "I can never remember who closes early and who stays late."

"I try to stay until seven most nights," I said. Nine seemed later than my shoppers would want to browse, and five was too early for folks who worked a regular day shift and wouldn't have time to stop by.

Mirabelle tugged her dog to the nearest chair, where she sat.

He collapsed on the floor at her feet, breaths heavy and tongue lolling.

I nabbed the bowl I kept handy for these occasions and filled it partway with water. "There you are, Mr. Dinky." I patted his head, and he rose in interest.

A narrow pink tongue coiled out at the sight of my offering, and he drank with gusto.

Mirabelle fished a notepad and pen from her oversized quilted handbag and crossed her legs at the ankles. "I've got personal and private business with you today," she said. "I have a few questions about Fryer's murder, and I want to buy Mr. Dinky a Christmas sweater."

She hefted a sizable pair of glasses from the chain around her neck and worked them up her snub nose. "There, now," she said, her milky eyes magnified. "Let's start with Fryer. What do you know about his murder?"

"Nothing, and not for lack of trying," I admitted.

"You've got to give me something," she said. "I only took

the crime reporting job because, until you came home, there wasn't any crime to report. Mr. Dinky and I ate cakes and watched our stories. Now, crime is rampant, I'm behind on all my shows and I'm up at all hours." She sighed, slumping back in the chair.

I wasn't sure I'd describe our local crime as rampant, and none of what she'd said was my fault, but I apologized anyway. "I'm sorry," I said, truly feeling bad for her. "I wish I could be more helpful."

Her eyes widened a bit. "You wouldn't want to trade jobs would you? I could watch the shop and you could do this." She extended the pen and paper in my direction. "You're already doing most of it anyway. You just don't write it down." Her brows rose with profound hope. "Do you write it down?"

"No." I shook my head. "Sorry. Have you considered retiring?"

She lifted and dropped her hands onto her lap. "Then what would I do? Eat cake and watch shows until I die? Who'd even know I was gone?"

I pursed my lips, unwilling to travel any further down that rabbit hole. "Maybe we should move on to choosing Mr. Dinky a sweater," I suggested.

"Wait." She straightened. "You really don't know anything?"

"Not really," I said, examining her a little more closely. "Why? What do you know?"

She shrugged. "Nothing about his death. Ask me something about his life."

"Was he married?" I asked. A wife wouldn't approve of a groupie. That seemed like solid motive, if his personality wasn't cause enough. "Maybe the wife killed him."

"Never married," Mirabelle said.

"Kids?"

She shook her head.

I thought of other people who might have a vested interest in someone's life and death. "How about a business partner?"

"Nope."

"Money troubles?"

She shook her head again. "Paid cash for Gnome Alone when he bought it from Vivian. Apparently he got an incredible deal."

My ears perked and my intuition tingled. "How good?"

"Good. That's all I know. Why?" she asked.

"I recently read somewhere that Fryer liked to lowball. You think he did that to Vivian?"

Mirabelle frowned. "Maybe. You want her number?"

"Yes, please."

She scribbled the digits on her notepad, then ripped the page off and handed it to me.

I smiled. "Thank you."

"Don't mention it," Mirabelle said. "Really. Don't tell her I gave that to you. She lives on Turtle Crossing. In case you want to pay her a visit."

"I'll call first," I said. "Thanks for giving Gigi Mr. Fryer's address the other night, but no one was home when I got there. You could put that in your article if you want."

I told her the rest of my story then. About the stolen carvings, cleaning every inch of Bless Her Heart in search of them, and writing the note. I kept the parts about Jean and the Road Crew to myself. I wanted a chance to see how things turned out tonight before folks read about it in the paper. "Who do you think will get all Fryer's stuff now that he's gone?" I asked. "No spouse. No kids. No business partner. What happens to our things if we have no one?"

Mirabelle looked infinitely sadder. "A few years ago, I would've said everyone has someone, but that's not always the case." Her gaze fell to Mr. Dinky, snoring softly at her feet. "Now I'm not sure what happens."

My heart broke a little. Did Mirabelle have anyone? Besides her dog? Extended family, children out of state? I couldn't remember hearing her talk about them.

I made a mental note to include her in my life more often and to reach out from time to time.

I refreshed my smile. "What color sweater would you like Mr. Dinky to have?"

She pushed onto her feet, eager to get started.

We moved through the store, examining clothes and trading stories about our busy days. I told her I'd used a trick she'd taught me last summer, to start seedlings in citrus rinds, and her smile warmed to new degrees. We held various sweaters up to Mr. Dinky, searching for the perfect color, and she suggested I have a house-warming party to celebrate my home when it was finished. I said I'd think about it, as long as she and Mr. Dinky promised to come.

Eventually, we found a website online for a pet boutique in New Orleans that would make anything Mirabelle wanted. So, I took her dog's measurements and helped her place an online order at the Furry Godmother. I bookmarked the page for later, when I could shop for Clyde.

"You said I only wanted a few jingle bells?" she asked, confirming I'd gotten the details correct. "I want my baby to feel festive, but I don't want to go overboard. Too many bells might frighten him when we walk, and he's too old to be startled."

"Got it," I promised. "Your package will be delivered in time for the holidays." The purchase hadn't exactly been budget friendly, but she said Mr. Dinky would only live once.

I walked them to the door and smiled as my mama pulled up to the curb and let Gigi out.

Gigi greeted Mirabelle, and the ladies chatted while Mama gave me a suspicious look.

Wide-set round headlights swung into place behind her, and Dad hopped out. "Hey, darling," he said, planting a kiss on my head. "Wish you could've come to dinner, but I'm glad to see you however I can." He dropped the truck keys into my hand. "Let me know if you buy something too heavy for you to lift. The employees at the store will help you get everything into the truck, but they won't follow you home to unload it. Your mama and I can help you with that."

"Thanks, Dad," I said, wrapping him in a tight embrace. "I'm on the hunt for wicker, so nothing should be too heavy. But I promise to call before trying to lift anything I think might be too much."

He smiled. "That's all I ask. Now, I'm off to take my sweetheart to a local vineyard. We're thinking of selling some dandelion wine at the farm."

"Good luck," I said.

Gigi moved to my side as Mirabelle and Mr. Dinky headed down the sidewalk.

Dad climbed behind the wheel of their truck.

Mama had slid to the passenger side and powered down the window. "You two be careful," she said, eyes flashing. "Y'all make up two-thirds of my heart. You hear me?"

Gigi and I nodded.

"Yes, ma'am," I said.

Mama sighed. "I'll see you tomorrow for the Makers Market."

I smiled.

"Gigi, will we see you for breakfast?" she asked.

"You betcha," Gigi said.

We waited for the truck's taillights to vanish before either of us spoke again. I exhaled a sigh of relief when they were gone.

"We really need to buy some patio furniture tonight," I said, swinging a guilty gaze to Gigi.

"Oh, I'm counting on it," she said. "What do you think of the outfit?" She turned in a circle, arms raised, before heading back into my shop.

She'd chosen a shiny silver blouse with cap sleeves and fitted black slacks with boots. "I thought I could borrow the motorcycle jacket from the rack," she said, already sloughing off her swing coat.

"Are you sure a silver blouse isn't too fancy for a diner?" I asked, completely out of my depth on this occasion.

"I'm also wearing leather," she said, attempting to roll the sleeves on a petite-sized coat.

I eyed my plaid maxi dress and denim jacket. "I need to change," I said, having not given any previous consideration to wardrobe for this theatrical event. "I'm borrowing jeans and a T-shirt to go with this jacket."

"Good idea," Gigi said. "What about your shoes?"

"I brought sneakers," I said.

Shoes were something I always thought about. And more recently, murderers.

"I want to be able to run if needed."

Gigi gave her boots a long look. "I think I'll stick with the boots. If someone chases us, you can get the truck and come back for me. Now, let's go meet some truckers!"

CHAPTER TEN

I said goodbye to Clyde, then hit all the switches near the door, leaving only the smattering of security lighting to keep my kitty company. He didn't mind. In fact, prowling around in the dimness, hidden by his sleek black fur, was his favorite mischievous activity. He especially enjoyed pouncing against the glass and terrifying unsuspecting dogs and their walkers.

"Be back soon," I told him as I stepped outside. "Don't give anyone a stroke while I'm gone."

Gigi double checked the lock with a moderate tug after I'd turned the deadbolt. "I thought we were taking the pickup," she said, frowning as I made my way to Marshmallow.

"We are." I reached into the car's trunk with both arms and hauled out a load of heavy, paint-spattered fabric. "But the truck says Bud's & Blossom's Flower Farm down both sides. I thought it might give away our real identities or direct a possible killer to Mama and Dad's doorstep."

She gave the truck another look, as if noticing the cheery, multicolored logo for the first time. "Good idea."

"Thanks. Lower the tailgate?"

She obliged, and I set my load on the sturdy metal ledge. "I brought all the drop cloths I had from painting the lake house, and some weights to hold them in place. We'll have to adjust once we get there, but we should do the bulk of the work now. Make it seems as if we're arriving in a work truck."

"We are," Gigi said.

I smiled. "Perfect."

We worked the materials strategically around the truck bed, hanging them out as needed to cover the logo and attempting to make the calculated angles appear haphazard to a stranger's eyes.

We dusted our palms, then high fived before getting into the cab.

Clyde watched from the window, his luminous eyes tracking our every move.

And Mason stood near the pub, one hand in his pocket, the other holding a take-out bag as we rolled away from the square.

The drive to Crossroads Diner took about twenty minutes, and a number of old trucks were lined up on the broken-concrete parking lot as promised. A collection of men sat around a series of picnic tables along the building's side, drinking from disposable cups and chuckling boisterously at their own banter. Zigzagged strands of bistro lighting bobbed overhead as external speakers piped "The Purple People Eater" into the night.

"Boy," Gigi said. "They all look really broken up about their loss."

"I was thinking the same thing." I pulled into a spot close enough for the men to notice my ride, and far enough away to avoid any unspoken invitations. We'd be fine as long as no one had a look under our tarps.

I followed Gigi inside to buy milkshakes and fries. She was full from a proper meal with my folks, and I was too nervous to eat more than a few bites while we were here. But there was always room for milkshakes.

We wandered out a few minutes later and pretended to look for open spots to sit and enjoy the evening.

Gigi moved to the nearest table with men on one side, backs turned to the empty bench, talking to men at the next table. "Are these seats taken?" she asked, smiling kindly as they turned.

A large man with visible forearm tattoos and an impressive beard narrowed his eyes. He wore a black band around one bicep, barely noticeable in the bunched material of his long-sleeve navy T-shirt, pushed up to the elbows.

Upon closer inspection, similar bands were visible on the other men as well.

"Sure," he said, approving after a long moment. "Tom," the man said, offering his hand.

"Susie," Gigi said. "This is my granddaughter, Dharma."

I turned a brittle smile in her direction.

Tom turned fully on the bench to face us, working his long legs under the table and resting meaty forearms on top. His friends from the other table peeked around to take a closer look.

"Beautiful names for beautiful women," Tom said.

Gigi made herself at home, fussing playfully with her hair. "Oh, stop."

I inhaled slowly, then sat. "You're all friends?" I asked.

"Yes, ma'am," Tom said. "We're a classic truck club. The Road Crew."

"That sounds fun," I said. "Do you race them?"

The group laughed. "Nah," Tom said. "We take good care

of them. They're collectors' items and pieces of history. Looks like you have a nice pickup of your own."

Gigi beamed. "We do. It was my husband's. He took great care of it until he passed. Now we take it out from time to time and reminisce."

I patted her arm, feeling the warmth of her words. "Grandpa loved that truck."

Tom smiled. "It's a beauty."

"Thank you kindly," Gigi said. "I know my husband would appreciate this club. Rest his soul."

I pointed to Tom's armband. "I hope that doesn't mean you've lost a friend."

His face sobered, as did the men's expressions around him.

Tom shifted. "A crew member passed unexpectedly yesterday."

"Oh, dear. We're so sorry for your loss," I said.

I looked to Gigi, unsure how to ask more about their fallen friend without giving us away.

She sucked on her milkshake straw and bopped her head to a song I didn't recognize.

I was on my own, and the silence was stretching.

Something new came to mind, and I felt a little icky. There weren't any women around, like there were in the Facebook photos. The men wore black armbands. Had Gigi and I unintentionally crashed a wake? Maybe they'd been laughing earlier because they were paying tribute to their friend.

I ate another fry, wishing I could crawl under the table, drag Gigi with me, then creep away unnoticed.

A tall man in a red flannel shirt and brown work pants exited the diner and moved in our direction. I hadn't noticed him inside when we ordered, but the place was busy. He smiled when he noticed us. "Well, hello," he said, hooking both thumbs behind his belt. "I leave these guys for a hot minute and two beautiful ladies arrive."

"Susie," Gigi said, pointing to herself, then me. "And Dahlia."

"Dharma," I said, correcting her when Tom's brows furrowed. "She's always teasing me like that."

Tom's answering smile was weak.

"I'm Turbo," the new guy said, moving to rest his hip on the table's end, inches from my shake and fries. He was older than the rest, easily Gigi's age. Thin and wiry. "These are my guys, Axel," he said, pointing to Tom. He turned slightly, shifting the aim of his finger from one man to the next as he assigned them names as well. "Vegas, Hawkeye, Gears, Rider and Blue."

My heart rate climbed at the sounds of their club names, raising the hairs on my arms over one name in particular. Tom, AKA Axel.

He'd been the one hashing out a beef with Mr. Fryer online until the group moderator was forced to turn off commenting for the post.

Gigi leaned in Turbo's direction. "It's nice to meet you. Are you all from around here?"

Turbo ran a hand over his mostly bald head and smoothed the ring of white hair just above his ears, then winked at her. "I've lived all over this country. Been to war. Traveled the globe. But there is nothing like life in southern Georgia to make my heart beat. I think it's all the peaches."

I grimaced.

Gigi purred. "Smooth talker."

"How would you like to check out my truck?" he asked, stretching a hand past my face to Gigi.

"Would I!" she said with impressive, hopefully false, enthusiasm.

I watched as she curled her fingers over the crook of Turbo's arm, and the pair meandered away.

"He's harmless," Tom said, apparently catching my expression. "He founded the club, so he was here when I joined. I've known him a few years now, and he's good people."

According to a murder suspect, I thought.

"Turbo is your leader?" I asked. The hierarchy of classic truck clubs being new to me.

Tom bobbed his head. "It's his baby, so it makes sense. Plus he has the time. Most of the rest of us are still juggling two jobs, raising kids and dealing with exes."

I pulled my gaze back to him, splitting my attention between the mission and Gigi as she walked the lot full of trucks with Turbo.

Tom chuckled. "I mean it," he said. "Turbo's a good guy. Your granny's in good hands."

A disbelieving smirk crossed my face before I could stop it. "Oh, trust me. If your friend tried anything Susie didn't like, it wouldn't be her I'd worry about."

His expression faltered, and I cleared my throat.

"Did you say you work two jobs?" I asked, hoping to wheel the conversation back to Mr. Fryer.

He nodded solemnly. "There's not a lot of work out there for laborers these days. Everyone wants a degree or certification of some kind, saying folks need formal training for a position. A solid work ethic and two good hands aren't enough to make ends meet anymore. Especially when a person's paying alimony and child support from marriages that went south." His jaw locked, and his gaze darted away before returning to meet my eye. "Not that you'd know anything about that, I'm sure."

"I don't," I said. "It sounds rough."

His hard eyes seemed to soften at my words. "It is. You ever been married?"

"I'm newly divorced," I said. "But I'm doing okay, and I don't have to pay alimony or child support, so that helps."

"Indeed it does."

I scanned the lot and the quiet men at the next table. My presence had clearly put the kibosh on their fun. "You're all collectors. Do you all have more than one?"

Tom rubbed a hand over his beard and looked away again.

"I don't know anything about trucks, but they're all so pretty and well maintained. You'd think it was the 1950s based on half of this parking lot. They shine like they're brand new. I'll bet they're worth a lot of money."

Tom's expression tightened further. The loose, easy smile he'd shown me earlier was long gone. "Most of us just have one," he said, gaze drifting over the vehicles. "Some guys buy them ruined and fix them up. Others have a ride that's been passed down and entrusted to our keeping by a friend or relative."

"You?" I guessed.

"I got mine from my grampy. I never had a father, and Grampy raised me like his own. We spent years together under the hood of his old truck. He taught me everything about her and her history. The things that pickup had seen and been through. Freedom rallies and memorial parades. Carrying Granny to the hospital to have my mama, then carrying Mama to the hospital to have me. I even carried him to the ER in it when his heart failed while we were fishing. It was the first vehicle he ever owned, and the one he took his last ride in."

I choked up, clearly imagining the story as he told it. The old pickup, the family ties, the history, were all things I related to deeply and truly. "Which is yours?" I asked, having temporarily forgotten the details of the dispute I'd read online between Tom and Mr. Fryer.

His giant hands curled into fists on the table. "She's not here. I had to sell her to make the mortgage payment at my ex-wife's house. I didn't want to do it, but it was either that or see her and the kids tossed out. And not for the first time. I used the money that was leftover on a lawyer, trying to get custody so I can make sure my money's going to the kids and their care, instead of whatever that nutcase woman does with it, 'cause it ain't paying the bills or keeping their bellies full."

My lips parted, but words failed.

Tom shook his head, gaze distant and expression grim.

"I'm sorry," I said, meaning it in my bones. What he'd described was awful, and it broke my heart. For him and his children. "Was the money enough to change things?" If it had been, I could at least tell him that maybe it was his grampy's way of looking out for him, even now.

"No." His Adam's apple bobbed, and he flicked his eyes to meet mine once more. "The man I sold it to was a known tightwad and a schemer. Always looking to take a little more and get a little extra. He knew the situation I was in, that no one else was in a position to buy, and that I didn't have time to list the truck properly and wait while folks drove down from all over to look at it. I needed money for a mortgage payment immediately. He knew I had to take what he offered. And he offered low. Real low. So, I was stuck between getting a fair price on something Grampy trusted me with or feeding my kids."

The quiet men behind him bobbed their heads but didn't make eye contact, move or speak. Clearly this was a story they'd heard before, and one that made them all a little uncomfortable.

"Your buyer doesn't sound like a very nice guy."

Tom's finger lifted to absently touch the band on his arm. "He wasn't, but karma's a b—"

"Yep," I said, cutting him a little short. "It is that. But you don't mean he's the one who passed unexpectedly, do you?" I gave his fingers on the band a pointed look.

A gleam flickered in his dark eyes, and he dropped his hand to his lap. "I offered to buy the truck back when I got on my feet again, and he told me he'd expect retail pricing. He wanted me to pay him more to get my truck back than he'd spent buying it from me." He pressed his lips together until his face turned red and his lips went white.

A yellow hatchback with one black door and a missing bumper rolled into the lot, classic country music blaring.

"Looks like the ladies have arrived," a man called from the next table. He pushed quickly onto his feet, and the other men followed suit. "Should've known Jeanie wouldn't miss a wake for Hotrod."

Tom's lips curved into a small smile. "About time her dad gave her a break." He rose, eyes fixed on the little car rounding the lot in search of a space near the row of trucks.

I jolted to my feet at the sound of her name, then checked my watch. We'd been at Crossroads for more than an hour. Where had the time gone? And how could we escape unseen by Jean? I waved frantically at Gigi. "Tom," I said, "I'm sorry to rush off, but I have to go. Emergency at home," I fibbed, cringing as I said the words. "Take care of yourself!"

She noticed immediately and dug a pen from her purse. She wrote something on Turbo's hand, then took off in my direction, sliding on loose gravel in her slick-bottomed boots.

I imagined getting the truck and spinning through the lot to grab her. Instead, I clutched her hand the moment she was in reach and nearly dragged her to the pickup, thankful for the mob of older men gamely greeting their groupie.

We dove into the pickup and high tailed it back toward Bliss in a cloud of dust and luck.

"Are you okay?" I asked Gigi, stealing glances at her as I put as much space as possible between us and the Road Crew.

"I'm great!" she said. "I haven't flirted like that in ages. It was shameless." She chuckled. "Kind of fun being someone else for a minute. And I think I liked that Turbo. I gave him my number. Do you think he'll call?"

I stared open mouthed at her for a long beat before pulling my eyes back to the road. "I don't know, Susie," I said. "What do you think?"

"Ah, dang it," she said. "I forgot I lied about my name."

"What did you think about Tom?" I asked. "I got bad, scary vibes from Tom. He had an excellent motive for confronting and lashing out at Fryer, and he's big enough to have knocked him dead without trying," I said. Sometimes people weren't maliciously violent. Sometimes they're just mad.

Regardless, just in case I was right, and considering his direct personal relationship with Turbo, Gigi might want to consider changing her number.

CHAPTER ELEVEN

I dropped Gigi off at her place, then circled back to the square to pick up Clyde. He was mad about his late dinner, and I'd barely eaten my fries. When I ran off, I'd accidentally left them and my shake on the picnic table outside the diner. So, I was also struggling with the reality of being a litter bug.

I pushed the tarps into the truck bed, uncovering the locally beloved logo, so nothing would seem amiss to anyone familiar with the pickup, then I left the vehicle outside Bless Her Heart, and took the marshmallow to pick up dinner. Walking alone at night, even in the statistically safe and friendly downtown, felt uncomfortable after the last couple of days. So, I drove to the other side of the square and parked outside the pub. The line was long, and the pub was crowded, but I didn't mind the wait. The food was worth it, and I enjoyed the energy buzzing around me. Plus, Clyde was safe inside my car and likely enjoying the night. The temperature had dropped to 65 degrees, and he was comfy in his sleek fur coat.

Nearly thirty minutes later, I'd ordered, paid and climbed

back into my car. "I got shredded chicken for you," I told him, "And a loaded baked potato for me."

I'd enjoyed my potato immensely the night before, but I'd been too hungry to savor it. Tonight, I would take my time, put my feet up and unwind. The painting was done. I could eat slowly, take a long, hot shower, then sleep. As long as my mind didn't keep me up, baking cakes and pies until dawn. I wasn't in the mood, and I was desperate for a single night off.

I practiced yoga breathing on the drive home, thankful for the vacant roads and a sky full of stars. The lack of street-lights near my home made it difficult to see anything outside my porch light's range, but that same darkness gave the sky everything it needed to take my breath away.

For practical reasons, I left my porchlight on anytime I'd arrive home after dark.

A strange flickering caught my attention as I neared the lake house, and I struggled to make sense of it upon approach. "Do you see that?" I asked Clyde, leaning closer to my wheel.

My driveway was empty when I arrived, but the glow of light behind my home sure seemed like a fire, possibly burning in my new firepit.

I wasn't about to confirm on my own, so I dialed Mason.

He swore quietly, then shouted that he was on his way.

Seven minutes later, his Jeep tore into view.

My body shook as I waited for him to park and climb out.

I'd driven up and down the street while I waited, sneaking enough peeks at my backyard to confirm the flames were coming from my patio firepit.

No need for the fire department or 911.

Mason walked to my car door and waited while I bumbled out. He curled me against his chest and pressed an unexpectedly protective kiss against my head, then released me in favor of taking my hand. "Let's take a look before we move Clyde inside."

My spluttering thoughts moved from the tender embrace to his consideration of my cat, and my dried-up heart grew a little more supple. "Okay."

Mason kept me behind him as we walked along the shadows of my home to the backyard and gazed at the now small flames. A pile of charred drop cloths hung from the pit's edges.

Mason put the fire out, then checked the house for signs of forced entry, while I freed Clyde and plated his chicken.

We returned to the patio so Mason could assess and document the crime scene while my potato went cold.

I sat in my Adirondack, stunned speechless and mentally floundering.

He looked over his shoulder at me as he photographed, then packed the cooled materials and ashes for evidence. "Tell me you're over there fully absorbing the calamity of this situation."

"No," I said honestly. It was more like my mind was working overtime to pretend none of the scary things I'd experienced lately had happened. It was ridiculous and unhealthy but true nonetheless. Each time my thoughts ventured toward the ugly things, it was as if my mind turned the wheel and skirted away. "Oh no," I whispered, a new and equally awful thing coming to mind.

"There you go," he said. "Finally."

I cupped my hands over my trembling lips. "I lied to my parents," I whispered. "I told them I needed the truck to buy new patio furniture, and I never even went to the store."

Mason lifted both arms at his sides and held the pose for several seconds before dropping them back at his sides. "That's what you're worried about right now? Patio furniture?"

"I don't like to lie to them," I said. "And they're going to want to kill me when they confirm their suspicions that I wasn't honest about my reasons for borrowing their truck."

"And what was the real reason?"

I bit my lip and averted my gaze.

"Look. I don't mean to be a total pill here, but there's a good chance whoever started this fire might want to actually kill you. So, I don't care why you lied to your parents, but you're going to have to start being straight with me right now. Whoever did this could've just as easily set your home on fire or your business. With you in it."

I shivered.

"I know," he said softly, mocking. "Sometimes, when I see a big hornets' nest, I too like to get real close, then kick it. Just to see what they'll do."

I gave him a heavy-lidded stare.

Mason gathered the evidence under his arm and offered me his hand. "I'm guessing these drop cloths are the ones from your folks' pickup truck. You had the flower farm logo covered pretty well when you drove past me on the square earlier. Probably on your way to sniff around somewhere you don't belong. See if you could peeve off a killer."

"Yep," I said. Accepting his hand and letting him pull me up. "Gigi and I went for burgers and shakes at Crossroads Diner."

He shook his head as he led me to my door.

"Whoever did this knows where I live, and they made it home before me," I said. "Is that possible?" I calculated the time I'd spent ordering and picking up dinner before driving home. The timeline was tight, but I supposed most things were possible.

"Someone must've been there when I left the truck, then used the small amount of time I was at the pub to swipe the tarps, come to my house and start a fire." It was the second time this week I'd been threatened while ordering takeout. Maybe Mason wasn't the only one who needed to start cooking.

He leaned against the house beside my door and watched me. "Given the latest turn of events, I'm going to have to insist you stay with your folks or Gigi while I figure this out. If Fryer's killer did this, then we know the perp has your name, address, place of work and details on your folks' business and home."

My jaw dropped. "I can't stay with any of them." The last time I'd gotten into this kind of mess with Gigi around, she wound up gagged and bound on her sofa. "They could get hurt because of me."

"Yeah," he said slowly. "I'm trying to be compassionate, but I'm so darn frustrated. Digging around in my murder investigations is a terrible idea. It gets you and people you love hurt. And it just makes no sense. But here we are again."

The sigh that followed his rant was thick with exhaustion. "Stay at Cami's then. Dale's there. He's trained to protect you. Honestly. I don't care where you stay, as long as it's not here."

I shook my head while he spoke. "There's no way I'm leading a lunatic to any of my loved ones' homes. And can I just add that whoever did this is completely jumping the gun? I've barely asked any questions."

Mason looked at my home, then at me and sighed again. "Why don't you stay at my place?" he asked woodenly, as if he hoped I would decline.

"Yes."

Most of me saw the awkward, uncomfortable nightmare a platonic night of personal protection at Mason's home could be. That part of me knew what the gossips would make of it, and that there wasn't any way to avoid being seen coming or going, unless he lived in a hut or under a bridge. The smaller curiosity-driven part of me did not care.

"Do you need to sit down?" he asked, steering me inside once the door was open. "You look paler than usual."

"I'm fine," I bluffed. "Just thinking about all the things I need to pack for a night away." I stubbed my toe on the threshold and nearly fell on Clyde.

Mason steadied me, then released me the second I regained my footing. "Sit. I'll get you some water while you plan what to pack." He returned with a bottle from my fridge.

My teeth began to chatter.

"What's going on with you?" he asked, opening the bottle before handing it to me. "Are you sick? What are you thinking?"

"I was wondering if you live under a bridge."

I gulped the water down, limbs trembling, and I realized I'd been in some kind of shock that was wearing off. The leftover adrenaline pounded through my veins, making me want to run, scream or fight something. I was in no shape to do any of that, so tears threatened to form.

"You think I'm homeless?" he asked, looking down at himself. "Is it the outfit or my personal hygiene?"

"No," I said between deep sips. "You smell really good."

He grinned. "I have a house," he said. "It's not under a bridge. It's nice and it has a guest room."

"Really?" The idea Mason didn't live in his Jeep, on the continuous lookout for criminals seemed strange.

"Yes, really," he said. "Where do you think Cat stayed when she was with me last summer?"

"Honestly, I'd tried not to think about that." Cat was a willowy blonde who'd visited a few months prior and introduced herself as his girlfriend, which had triggered some kind of cavewoman reaction in me. It was jealous and overprotective, nothing like I'd ever felt before, and I didn't like it. So, I didn't think about that either.

He took a seat beside me, brows furrowed. "Why do you

still look so shocked? I've been here for months. Did you think I lived in my Jeep?"

I chewed my lip. "Kind of. Or maybe in a studio apartment over a butcher shop or something."

"No," he said, making a crazy face.

"Okay, so where do you live?" I asked.

I set the empty bottle on my coffee table and waited, suddenly needing the answer to this question like I needed oxygen.

Mason focused on the discarded bottle, his frame suddenly tense, as if he was in trouble. "Not too far from here."

I blinked. "You live on the lake?" I asked.

He'd never mentioned that before. Was he one of my neighbors? Did he live within walking distance? I'd been meaning to start a regular walking routine. Fitness was important.

"Yeah."

I stared at his forehead until he raised his eyes to mine. "Where on the lake?"

"You should get your things together," he said. "And Clyde's. Is there anything I can do to speed this up?"

I pushed onto my feet, warmed again by his compassion for my kitty. "Fine. I'll go without any more questions but only because I want to be sure you don't sleep under a bridge."

"Planning to see where I sleep already?" Mason asked, turning a cheeky grin in my direction.

And I knew I'd regret this in the morning.

CHAPTER TWELVE

*W*e took Lake Drive in a long curving sweep to the east. Mason at the wheel of his open-top Jeep, Clyde and I freezing in the passenger seat. Our bags tucked neatly in the back.

I squinted through the darkness at the sporadic homes and long wooden docks stretching into the water. "I can't believe you live on the lake and never told me."

"You didn't ask," he said. "And in fairness, I tried to bring the subject up once, when you were house hunting, but you got all dramatic and shut me down."

I gasped and pressed a palm to my collarbone. "I am not dramatic."

He rolled his eyes.

"Wait," I said, a swell of panic rising in my chest as a familiar sign whizzed past. "That was the city limit." I craned around on my seat, staring blankly behind us. "You've left our village. There." I pointed to the next visible street. "You can take the next left and head back. No. Now, you must've missed the turn."

Mason didn't speak or reduce our speed.

"You missed the turn," I repeated, glaring as the Welcome to Cromwell sign flashed into view then blurred past.

I dragged my eyes to Mason. "You missed it. Right?"

"Nope."

My jaw dropped, and for a moment, I considered jumping from the vehicle. "You live in Cromwell?" I squeaked. "Are you kidding me?" I stage whispered, checking to see if anyone was watching from passing cars or their nearby homes. I flipped my sweatshirt's hood over my head for added anonymity.

"That's not at all dramatic," Mason said. "Or ridiculous in any way."

"Shush, you," I complained. "You know what will happen if I'm spotted over here."

He stared down at me. "Yes. In my experience, someone will wave."

I worked to close my mouth as we whipped through the night, and I thought about his position as the sheriff. We had discussed his jurisdiction before; that was true. And while the sheriff's department was located in Bliss, his duties and services extended to cover the entire county, which included Cromwell. He'd mentioned before that Cromwell's local police force was typically all the law enforcement they needed, but if anything came up that required more man power, the sheriff's department would step in.

"Listen," he said. "I'm trusting you with this information. I know how weird everyone in your village gets about some old rivalry between towns, but I didn't know that when I bought my place. I needed something fast and within my budget, so I moved on the deal. Now it's my home, and apparently that's wildly offensive to a good portion of the civilians in my protection. So, I'd appreciate it if you could keep this to yourself."

I gripped the dashboard as we left the road, bouncing

over lumpy grass toward the water. "What are you doing?" I asked, suddenly concerned he might drive us into the lake if I don't agree.

The Jeep halted with a jolt as Mason parked near the weeds at the end of a long dock with a large rectangular boat stationed at the end.

There weren't any homes around, and we hadn't passed any in a while.

He climbed out and gathered my things from the back.

"Where are we going?" I asked, clambering down with Clyde in his carrier and hustling to meet Mason at the dock.

"Home." He tipped his head toward the boat and strode away on the old wooden boards.

I scanned the night, wondering if anyone could see us, and a little thrill shot down my spine. I was sleeping over at Mason Wright's house. *In Cromwell.*

The scandal of it all made me feel twenty years younger, fizzy and alive. All I needed was a little stolen hooch from a friend's parents' fridge and a few rock ballads, and I would be skinny dipping by midnight.

"You coming?" Mason asked, and the concept of skinny dipping went right out my mental window.

Gravity had not been my friend these last few years, and I no longer went anywhere without the proper equipment holding things up and in.

"Watch your step," he said, helping me onto the boat by my elbow.

The electricity of his touch rolled over my skin, standing the fine hairs along my arm on end.

He released me quickly once more, just the way he had at my place. "You can set Clyde free whenever you're ready, and I'll give you the ten-cent tour."

I released my furry companion immediately, and he stood on widespread legs. "It's a boat," I told him. The movement of water beneath us was subtle, but Clyde seemed to notice and was unsure. "You'll get used to it," I promised.

"This is the living area and kitchen," Mason said, flipping switches on the wall.

A neutrally decorated living space with a small seating arrangement, lamps and end tables stood before a narrow galley kitchen. The areas were separated by an island with stools and a change from carpet to tile flooring. Windows lined every wall around the living room, each with a curtain that dragged the floor. Based on the interior and décor, the boat had likely originated at some point in the decade before I was born.

I peeked outside.

The area beyond the glass was covered by an awning and contained a patio set and grill.

"Would you rather walk the deck first?" Mason asked.

"No." I turned and hurried in his direction, eager to see more. "Just taking it all in."

A long hall lined in doors led to the other end of the boat. Two of the doors were small bedrooms. One was a bath. Three stairs led to a master suite below the space with an instrument panel and captain's chair.

I took note of the tidiness. The distinct lack of socks on the floor or dirty dishes in the sink. No signs of the endless take-out boxes and bags I always saw him with.

A short bookcase stood beside his bed, serving double duty as a night stand. An alarm clock and charging station was positioned on top, easily within reach of a sleeping Mason.

The mental image of Mason in bed caused a surge of heat to my cheeks, and I turned in the other direction to veil my reaction. I'd only managed to drum up the idea of a bare arm, back and shoulders before my heart began to race. There was something so intimate about the imagined mussed hair and heavy-lidded eyes, that I felt instantly like a creeper, though I hadn't meant to imagine it at all.

"Have you eaten?" Mason asked, completing my tour.

"No." I shook my head, then took the lead back to his kitchen, attempting to collect my marbles in the process.

"How do you feel about chicken salad on a croissant?" he asked, opening his fridge and peering inside. "I also have pasta salad and actual salad-salad, if you want a side dish. Actually, I have veggies from the farmers' market, but I can cut them into a salad pretty quickly."

I stared. "When was there a farmers' market?" My folks would surely have been there, front and center with Petal Pusher. They hauled their traveling flower cart to every craft fair and artisan event in town.

Mason grimaced, and I remembered where we were.

"You went to a Cromwell farmers' market," I said. The words came out a little breathless and unintentionally chastising.

I took a beat to consider the level of offense eating Cromwell veggies would mean to my town, then decided I was too hungry to make a proper evaluation. "A chicken-salad sandwich sounds perfect."

Mason gathered his materials, then snagged a bag of chips from the cabinet. He assembled two sandwiches and delivered them to me at the island. "What can I get you to drink?"

"You live on a boat," I said. "On the wrong side of the lake."

"Beer?" he asked, reaching back into the fridge for two brown bottles with a man in a fedora on the front.

"I guess. But you live on a boat," I repeated. "In Cromwell."

He uncapped the bottle and set it beside my plate. "I'm aware."

I didn't usually drink beer, but the bottle had my attention. The label said it was made by the Great Lakes Brewing Company and the beer's name was Eliot Ness. It seemed strangely appropriate, so I took a ginger sip.

"Ness was the safety director in Cleveland during the mid 1930s," Mason said. "Cleveland was the fifth-largest city in our nation back then and widely considered to be the most dangerous."

I smiled. "An idol of yours?"

Mason's answering expression was youthful and a little unsure. "Maybe."

We settled into our meal, tension falling away and the reality of my situation sinking in. I was on Mason's houseboat. In the months since I'd met him, he'd never mentioned where he lived or invited me over, and I'd never given his home much thought. He always seemed to pop up at my place, usually with food, and that was incredibly convenient.

"What do you think?" he asked.

I wasn't sure if he meant the beer or the boat, but I liked one more than the other.

There was something about the water all around us, visible through a wall of windows and open curtains, moonlight rippling over lapping waves, that made the simple sandwiches feel more personal than any meal at my place ever had.

He watched me chew, then swallow, examining my wild hair and eyes.

I watched him in return.

I was mesmerized by his presence. Enchanted by his ridiculously handsome face and endearing grin. I could see his mental wheels turning, and I suspected there was something he wanted to say to me.

There was something I needed to tell him too.

I knew about the death of his ex, Ava. He'd fallen for her while working undercover as part of a joint task force with the FBI, and she'd discovered his truth. But she'd loved him too and refused to talk when her criminal group confronted her. They'd killed her, assuming she was the rat they'd suspected. And she'd let them. She didn't tell.

And Mason carried the weight of that with him. Of her death. His loss. And the guilt of knowing he'd been the catalyst.

"Bonnie," he said, his cautious blue gaze flicking from my eyes to my lips, then back. The sound of my name on his tongue, low and gravelly and sweet, made my head spin.

I curled my fingers around the countertop's edge to stop myself from swooning onto the floor.

"I think we need to talk," he said. "Not about what you've been up to or what happened to Mr. Fryer. I think we need to talk about us." His attention fell to my mouth again, and I panicked.

"I know what happened in Cleveland."

He pulled back, sitting taller and frowning. "What do you mean?"

"I know you fell in love with a woman named Ava," I began.

His eyes widened in horror and he leaned farther away as I wet my suddenly dry lips and forced myself to carry on, spilling the story as I understood it, and hating myself for keeping the secret so long.

His Adam's apple bobbed, and his cheeks darkened with shame. His gaze darted wildly before resting on me once again.

"And I needed you to know I know."

"Wha—" He slid off the stool and onto his feet, looming over me in all his unfair height. "How?" He stepped back and bumped into the wall. "How can you— I don't under—"

"Dale," I said, explaining everything with a single word.

Dale worked for the FBI team assigned to the task force. It was how the men became friends.

Mason ran a hand over his head, scraping unsteady fingers through his hair. "I...uhm..." He turned in a circle. "I have to go. I got a call, and I need to go, but you should stay. Eat. Make yourself at home. I'll be back when I can." He walked a crooked line through his living space and to the door where we'd come inside.

"Wait," I called, stumbling belatedly after him. "Mason! Stop! Talk to me."

His long legs ate up the dock to his truck in half the number of strides it would've taken me. And he didn't look back.

I didn't bother trying to give chase.

What would I say if I caught him?

The headlights of his Jeep flashed over the side of his boat, and I watched helplessly as he reversed in a sharp circle, tearing up the grass and leaving a donut of mud and earth in his wake.

I locked the door behind him and scooped Clyde into my arms.

We couldn't leave if we wanted to. It wasn't safe to walk alone at night, and we were too far from home to try.

So, I cleaned up our dinner, then cried myself to sleep.

CHAPTER THIRTEEN

I wasn't sure when Mason came home, but he was up and showered when I crawled out of bed just after dawn. He fed me toaster waffles and coffee without speaking more than two words at a time, then he drove me back to my place, where I could get ready for the day and drive myself to work.

I didn't blame him for not wanting to talk to me, and I didn't push him.

I'd ambushed him with my significantly overdue confession and blurted the details of what was possibly his darkest, or most shame-filled, secret. I'd clawed the scab off a still-healing wound and unearthed all that pain and grief with a few simple sentences.

Not to mention I'd derailed whatever he'd been working himself up to say to me.

But I was glad he finally knew I knew.

I applied lip gloss in front of my bedroom mirror and sighed at the reflection staring back. My sunflower yellow dress was vintage, cheery and bright. With a little luck, it would soon improve my mood, as great outfits often could.

The thing that bothered me most about my confession was whether I'd done it for the right reason. Had I said all those things so abruptly to clear the air before Mason said whatever he'd been about to say? Or had I self-sabotaged because I wasn't ready to hear him?

Clyde leaped onto the dresser, as if sensing my dismay. He rolled onto his back and peered up at me, furry kitty paws in the air.

"I might need a counselor," I said, knowing I absolutely did. "I've been through a lot since I moved home, but Grant really messed me up before that, and now it's all become too much, and I might be messing myself up."

Clyde purred and reached for me with one paw.

"I'm serious," I told him. "It's been a year since I moved home and a decade since Grant touched me or looked at me longer than necessary." I hadn't been in love with him those last few years, but the intentional silence and lack of connection had still felt like abuse. "I've been on my own a long time," I told Clyde. "And Mason really is nice. He's my friend and a good guy. So why am I so afraid he might care about me the way I care about him? And why would I never admit my feelings for him to anyone but you?"

Clyde wriggled, then rolled onto his fluffy tummy.

"Well, obviously," I said, stroking his soft fur. "You're my best friend, and I tell you everything."

He was handsome as always in his little yellow bow tie and bell.

Our ensembles were perfectly coordinated.

I smoothed my dress and lifted my chin. I had my faults, but I was working on them, and that was all that mattered.

"Let's go," I told Clyde. "We'll call Latiesha when we get to work." My former marriage counselor knew me well and might have contacts in my area. With a little luck, I'd soon be working on myself from the inside out.

The Volkswagen seemed to have a mind of its own as we left for work. We motored along Lake Drive without making the necessary turn toward town, moving instead toward the boat where I'd spent the night in Cromwell.

Part of me wanted to see I hadn't imagined it, and that it was still there, even when Mason wasn't. A quick drive by assured me the boat was real, and I wasn't imagining things, but it didn't make me feel any better.

I stuck to the more obscure roads on my return trip to Bliss. The last thing I needed was to be spotted across enemy lines. The only problem was that it didn't take long for me to get lost.

"This is what I get," I told Clyde. "I pressed my luck, entering Cromwell twice in twelve hours, and now I'm driving in a circle."

It took several false starts and do-overs before the GPS finally rescued me, apparently equally confused by the labyrinth of twisty, hidden roads on the other side of the lake.

A sigh of relief slipped from my lips as a familiar residential intersection came into view. "We're home, Clyde," I said. "Back in Bliss, where we belong." Thank my lucky stars.

A large yard sale appeared in the distance, and my rattled brain snapped to attention. We were less than a hundred yards from Mr. Fryer's home, which looked completely different in the daylight.

When I'd dropped by to deliver the carvings, his old farmhouse had seemed menacing and eerie. By the light of a morning sun, it was almost charming with its porch swing and old pickup parked out front. I drove past it to the yard sale at the house next door.

A number of cars lined the curb and gravel drive that ran parallel to Fryer's. I added my Volkswagen to the count.

"How about a little thrift shopping?" I suggested to Clyde.

He yawned and stretched in a shaft of sunlight spilling into his crate, clearly disinterested.

I checked the temperature on my dashboard, then powered down the windows. "I'll be right back. Holler if you need me."

I walked the driveway between properties, scoping out Mr. Fryer's home as I moved. Remembering the way I'd stood on the porch, knocked on the door and waited. There was an unnatural creaking sound, but no signs of a second doorway or wooden boards nearby. Just the porch where I'd stood and knocked.

Where Fryer's body was later discovered.

A cool breeze jingled windchimes hung from a massive reaching oak in the neighbor's yard, drawing me into the sprawling sale. Pale paper tags on thin brown strings floated and hovered like kites on the wind, declaring the price to each of a hundred items. Books and dishes. Table and chair sets. Old records and clothes. It was the kind of sale that would've gotten my heart pumping if I wasn't so distracted by the nearness of a recent murder site.

The deeper I moved among the things, the better view I had of Mr. Fryer's property as a whole. Neatly cut green grass had been mowed in crisscross lines. Tidy mulch ringed his home, just like his business on the square. A single outbuilding sat out back, freshly painted and adorned with an old metal gas station sign.

All around me, however, was chaos. Stuff upon stuff. Furniture under trees. Tables of knickknacks and rolling racks of old clothes. The view from his place must've been awful.

I craned my neck to peer along the side of the house before me, straining to inspect the backyard for signs of additional clutter. I wasn't disappointed. Chicken coups, pens and outbuildings spilled their contents across the brown lawn and invisible property line, delineated currently by the end of Fryer's lush green grass.

"Yikes," I whispered, suddenly reevaluating the home before me.

The large stone structure had clearly been a mansion in its day, with wide sweeping porches and windows with sills deep enough to stand in. The place was in need of basic maintenance, but given the state of the lawn, it seemed reasonable to assume the current owner wasn't a fussy sort or concerned with upkeep.

A large metal lantern and stack of old books with thread-bare pastel covers caught my eye, and I piled them immediately into my arms. No sense missing out on a deal while I poked around. *And the shopping is an excellent cover*, I reasoned.

"Welcome," a woman in baggy jeans and an oversized T-shirt called from the porch. She appeared to be my age, give or take a few years. Her skin was suntanned, her lips were thin. And she appraised me with an abundantly cautious smile.

A few browsers raised their hands and voices in returned greetings.

The woman's gaze caught on me, and she headed in my direction, arms open as if she might hug me. When she began to turn in a small circle, I realized this was more of a *behold my wares* move. "Let me help you," she said, stopping to sweetly take the lantern from my grip. "You need those hands open so you can shop."

"Thanks."

She wedged the stack of books beneath one bent arm and scrutinized me with sharp brown eyes. "I'll keep these in the foyer by my register," she said. "You just take your time and give me a shout if you have any questions."

I smiled and a dozen questions piled on my tongue. *Where*

was she on the night Mr. Fryer was killed? Did she see or hear anything unusual that evening? Did she know her neighbor well? Had he behaved strangely the last few days? Did he have any enemies she knew of? What had the police done so far in their investigation of the property?

My lips clamped shut, knowing better than to show my hand too soon and scare her away. Or unintentionally deliver more fodder for the local gossip mill. Instinct kept me from letting her get away.

"I own a shop on the square," I said, hurrying along after her. "I sell old things like these. I bought a pair of silver lamps here once."

She slowed to look over her shoulder. "Oh?"

I nodded. "Yeah, I'm going to use these books in a display. I'll sand and repaint the lantern a bright pastel color, maybe periwinkle or pink."

She frowned.

"It seems like you've made quite a business from this yard sale. Lots of shoppers. Very impressive." I smiled in what I hoped looked like camaraderie, one female entrepreneur to another.

The woman shook her head. "It's just a yard sale. Businesses require permits, commercial property and documentation of income for tax purposes. My sale comes and goes periodically. A few hours a day here and there."

I performed an exaggerated stage wink. "Gotcha."

Her frown deepened.

This wasn't going the way I'd hoped. I needed to bond with the woman to ask such pointed, personal questions about her neighbor. As it was, it looked more like she might ask me to leave.

"Okay," I said, lifting my hands as we stopped at the base of an impressive wooden staircase. "You got me. I'm actually here because I heard about what happened to Mr. Fryer." I shrugged apologetically. "It's just so awful, and I'm trying to make sense of it. You know?"

The woman folded her arms. "Now we're getting somewhere. I'm Alyssa Sternman."

"Bonnie," I said. "Balfour."

"Oh, I know who you are," Alyssa said. "I read the papers. I knew the moment I saw you in my yard, staring at the Fryer place."

My mouth opened, but I shut it, unsure how to proceed.

"Before you hear it from someone else, if you haven't already, I didn't like Fryer. We didn't get along, and it's no secret. He came over here every chance he could to tell me my chickens crossed some imaginary boundary or my sale was encroaching on his property. He's got all that yard, and he doesn't even use it. It's maddening." She huffed and tallied up my items. "You probably came here to look at me as one of your suspects. Everyone in the yard probably knows it, so you're buying these things, and you're going to make it look like you're just shopping."

I passed Alyssa more than enough cash to cover my costs and tried for a patient smile. "I'm not here to accuse you of anything," I said. "Really."

Though, I couldn't stop thinking about the other note I'd seen on Mr. Fryer's notepad. There was something about a surveyor. Was he planning to push back about their property line?

Alyssa glared, and I wondered, nonsensically, if she could read my mind.

"You can keep the change," I said, hoping to make peace, especially if she was a killer.

"I planned on it."

I took the books and lantern, then a baby step backward, smile faltering. My mind raced with possibilities of what all the new information might mean. "Thank you for these things. I can't wait to see them in my new home." I definitely wouldn't resell them now. The look on her face suggested she might hunt me down and beat me with them.

"Don't mention it."

I hurried back to my car, smiling fondly at anyone making eye contact. I hadn't come here looking for a new suspect, but I'd definitely found one.

If Alyssa knew Fryer planned to have their property lines surveyed, and potentially reinforced, how mad would that have made her? She'd already admitted to not liking him. Would the attention caused by the survey bring an end to her "yard sale"? Was the sale her main source of income?

If so, would endangering her livelihood make her mad enough to kill?

CHAPTER FOURTEEN

The town square was aflutter with activity when I arrived for work. Massive signs and banners had been stretched between light posts and hung from the gazebo's roof, announcing the Makers Market. Dozens of local vendors had already set up shop, arriving early to secure the most coveted spots.

I freed Clyde inside Bless Her Heart, then headed for my office.

I'd saved two large boxes of materials especially for this event. Folks would begin evaluating our shop windows and storefront décor today, and I needed to impress.

I wedged my hip against the open front door as I dragged everything onto the sidewalk.

My antique red Radio Flyer wagon nearly overflowed with vanilla candles, mistletoe and décor asking folks to Give Thanks. I parked my childhood ride beside a tufted bench with neatly folded throw blankets and a row of coordinating pillows. Next, went my favorite rolling rack, showcasing an assortment of flashy wraps, party dresses and cuddly-looking cardigans. A variety of lanterns, my newest purchase excluded, completed the overall look.

Mouthwatering aromas rose from a line of food trucks and vendor carts, reaching my nose with promises of all things good and holy. Warm Belgian waffles smothered in sliced apples, cinnamon and whipped topping. Crepes stuffed with cream cheese and pumpkin spice.

My stomach grumbled, unapologetically furious about the lackluster breakfast I'd eaten in silence on Mason's boat. My stomach wanted the good stuff.

Cinnamon rolls, it moaned. *Sticky buns. Strudel.*

I checked my watch and weighed my options. Lexi was due in soon. Until then, I had to be strong.

I slipped back into my shop and checked on the shoppers who'd filtered in as I set up the sidewalk sale. Assured all was well, I brought up the village website on my phone and hunted for their planning department. My eyes spotted a number to the main office, and my fingers dialed before I could stop them.

I just couldn't stop thinking about that note Mr. Fryer had made about a survey. And I couldn't help wondering if the survey had something to do with his death.

My shoppers chatted merrily, paying me no attention as I listened to the tinny rings. I had no idea what I planned to say, but I figured the words would come when I needed them. I was learning to perform better under pressure these days.

"Village Planning," a chipper voice answered. "How can I direct your call?"

"Good morning. I'd like to talk to someone in the surveyor's office about a...survey." I cringed, wishing I'd thought that statement through before delivering it.

"One moment, please." The voice replied and was instantly replaced with elevator music.

The bells over my door jingled, and I waved to an influx of smiling faces. Their cheeks were rosy from the cool morning air. Shopping bags hung from their fingertips as they slowly filled the store. The decibel of chatter and soft giggles caused me to stick a finger in one ear.

A recorded message pulled my attention back to the phone, and a slow male voice recited instructions for me to leave a message for the village Department of Civil Engineers.

"Hello," I said, pausing to think up a plan. "I'm calling about the previously scheduled appointment for this week at 1135 Good Luck Lane. If someone could give me a call back, I would greatly appreciate it." I rattled off my name and phone number, then hoped whoever got the message wouldn't overthink my connection, or lack thereof, to the property before calling back.

Meanwhile, I had to figure out what to say when or if they did.

Lexi swept into view a moment later, fingers curled around a cup that smelled distinctly of warm apple cider. "Hey!" she said, spotting me as she tucked her bag behind the counter. "Great turnout this morning. Did you see the square? This is going to be our biggest sales day yet. I can feel it."

She cracked the lid off the cup, and my mouth watered. "Peggy and Stan are here from the orchard with a dozen kinds of apples, pies, turnovers and cider. It smells like I could gain twenty pounds just crossing the street. I think I saw six food vendors from the county fair and at least as many food trucks."

"It's setting up to be a great day," I agreed.

Lexi moved into place behind the register as shoppers began to line up at the checkout.

I walked to the window slowly, taking in the fantastic

show of locals, both buying and selling. Baby-clothes design-
ers, soap and lotion makers. Home décor and handmade-
jewelry booths. Plus tables with representatives from
photography studios, party venues and the local vineyard.
My folks would likely arrive any minute with Petal Pusher.

My attention snagged on a woman in a pointy red hat,
and I dragged my focus back to her booth. The white skirt
around her table bore a familiar and beloved logo. Gnome
Alone.

"Lexi?"

"Yeah?"

"I'll be right back." I hurried through the door and across
the street, careful not to be hit by a car while blatantly
jaywalking. Then I beetled over the grass to the Gnome
Alone stand.

The woman in the funny hat looked up as I approached.
"Bonnie!" Her green eyes danced with delight.

My pace slowed, suddenly unsure. This woman knew my
name too? Just as Alyssa Sternman had? That encounter
hadn't gone nearly as well as I'd hoped, so I said a silent
prayer that this conversation would be more productive. And
the woman less hostile.

Her smile waned. "You are Bonnie Balfour," she said.
"Right? Bud and Blossom's daughter?"

I relaxed a bit as I finished my trip to her side. "Yes. Sorry.
You know my parents," I said breezily. "That's great."

"I do," she said. "I used to babysit your mama. I'm only a
few years older, but when you're young, the difference
between sixteen and twelve is immense." Now that she'd said
so, she seemed my mama's age. Her shoulder-length brown
hair was heavily peppered with gray and worn in that long,
bobbed style of someone who could easily be a grandmama,
but wasn't ready to accept it.

I laughed. "I suppose it is. I hope she didn't give you any trouble."

"Never. Blossom loved to take walks and sit in the gardens. An utter delight then and now. How is she doing?" she asked. "I expected to see her today."

I looked around the crowded square. "She and Dad are good. They should be here soon with Petal Pusher."

"Wonderful!" she returned, eyes bright. "This is my first time setting up shop like this." She motioned to the gnome-themed wares around her. "I used to have a store over there, but I sold to The Truck Stop." Her expression flattened and she signed the cross. "Rest his soul."

"I heard about that," I said, thrilled to not have to bring the subject up awkwardly. Maybe this was going to be a good-luck day. "I'm sorry I never had the chance to shop while you were open. I was gone so many years. Some days it feels as if I missed everything. I've been all wrapped up in getting the doors open at Bless Her Heart since I moved home."

She waved me off. "Don't worry about it. Believe me. I know." She extended her hand to me for a gentle shake. "I'm Vivian Danvers."

"It's nice to meet you." I lifted a fat stuffed gnome door stopper, feigning nonchalance. "I guess it's hard to stop doing what you love."

"It is," she said, fussing a little with her hat. "I sank my heart and soul into Gnome Alone, and it was enough, until my youngest got into Wharton. She wanted to study business. Said I inspired her." Vivian beamed. "Heaven knows my kids all spent their share of time at my store when they lived at home. After school and on weekends when I couldn't find or afford a sitter, then working there when they were old enough to give me a break. Being a single parent is tough, but we all made it out alive." She laughed. "I sold the shop and as much inventory as possible so I could help my daughter with her expenses. I had a little nest egg to live on without the store, so I'm managing with that."

My heart melted. "You gave up the thing you loved for your little girl."

"I would give the heart from my chest if it meant one of my children would live another healthy, happy moment," she said. "There wasn't any choice to make. She was accepted to Wharton. Wharton! The first in my family to go to college anywhere, and she went straight to the Ivy League. I did everything I could to make that dream possible."

"Selling the store helped?"

She tipped her head over one shoulder, then the other, her expression saying there was a story there. "I wish I'd have gotten a better deal, but time was of the essence, you know? Schools like Wharton don't wait while prospective students' parents count and roll their pennies."

"You had to sell for less than the place was worth," I guessed. It wasn't a big leap, given what I knew about her buyer, Mr. Fryer, and what he'd done to his friend Tom.

Vivian stared, apparently stunned by my presumption.

"Sorry," I said, lifting a palm in apology. "You said you wished you'd gotten a better deal. I thought that might mean you were lowballed."

I waited on pins and needles for her response. If Fryer had shorted her too, it could be considered a pattern of behavior.

Her furrowed brows eased by a fraction. "My store was worth more than the offer I accepted. That's true, and it's on me, I suppose. I was being emotional, thinking like a mom who wanted to help her baby however she could. I felt the pressure to sell quickly, so I did." She shook her head. "And you can't blame a vulture for being a vulture. Swooping in on injured prey is what they do."

Her gaze flicked to The Truck Stop, and mine followed.

"Maybe you can get the space back now," I said. "If you wanted it."

She nodded. "Would if I could, but the loss left me in a pickle. I'm not sure I'd be able to manage the costs of a storefront now. But karma…" She pressed her lips together, possibly fighting a grin. "She knows your gnome."

"I should get back," I said. "I just wanted to say hello."

And add you to my suspect list.

"Take care of yourself," she said, all humor gone from her voice.

I shivered as a cold breeze blew in.

The wind ruffled the skirting on her table, and a silver serving tray came into view, tucked out of sight with a few boxes and bags. One little paper price tag on a string danced against it.

I froze, and my gaze darted back to Vivian, who watched me closely. "Do you know Alyssa Sternman?"

"Not personally," she said. "Why?"

I shook my head and smiled, hoping to look nonchalant. "I ran into her earlier. I guess she has a big yard sale that everyone loves. Another female entrepreneur. Maybe we should start a club."

"Or a support group," Vivian said.

"That's so funny," I said, unable to laugh, and certain my smile had slid from pleasant to unhinged. "She seemed very nice."

Vivian scanned the crowd and motioned me back to her with one curling finger. "She lives beside the Fryer place, and covers her lawn every day with a massive yard sale. I'll bet he woke every morning cursing her name."

"I've heard it's quite a sale," I said.

"I'm sure he hated it. He was such a neatnik. And a complainer. I didn't know much about him before he bought my shop, but I looked into him a lot afterward. With all my kids out of the nest, and no shop to run, I had plenty of time to check him out."

"And he was a complainer?" I asked.

She nodded slowly, eyebrows high. "Alyssa and Fryer fought all the time about her sale and their property line. I know it isn't nice, but it gave me a little pleasure knowing his life wasn't perfect once he'd taken my shop. I almost felt bad for him a few times. Rumor has it Alyssa can be ruthless."

"Interesting." I mentally rehashed the possibility Alyssa might've offed her neighbor. Then wondered if Vivian had a nefarious reason for attempting to plant that seed. "Do you think Alyssa could've gotten mad enough to confront him physically?"

Vivian blanched. Her mouth opened, then shut without speaking. She stretched back in her chair, visibly uncomfortable and distancing herself from the question.

"Sorry," I apologized again. "I get carried away."

"I guess we all have our things," she said, but her gaze moved over the square, avoiding contact with me and silently ending our discussion.

"Well, I hope you sell a lot today," I said, setting the doorstop down and patting his head. "Good luck."

Vivian smiled. "You too."

CHAPTER FIFTEEN

*C*ami's laugh broke through my silent discomfort, and I clocked her several booths away.

She looked as if she'd just walked off a runway, as usual, in a flattering red wrap dress and heels. Her hair was sculpted into a perfect French twist, showing off her long slender neck and admirable collar bones. I glanced at my dress, the boat neck drooping slightly from my poor posture.

I hustled to her side, trying to stand a little taller. "Hey!" I shouted over the local jug band.

Her eyes met mine, and her smile fell. She patted the table before her, then excused herself from the conversation. "I am so sorry," she said when she reached my side. "I've meant to check in with you all day."

"Mason came to see Dale?" I guessed.

She nodded, pulling me away from the booths for a measure of privacy. "I hate how poorly that went for you. You did a brave thing telling him. Whatever else happens, know that."

"I don't feel brave," I said. "I feel horrible."

She gripped my biceps gently, offering a sad but under-standing smile.

"What happened when he got to your place?" I asked, suddenly desperate to know.

"Dale spoke to him privately in my driveway," she said. "I watched from the window. There were lots of big hand gestures and a constant rumble of voices. Whatever they said, it got heated before it got better."

"But it got better?" A flicker of hope rising in my chest. "Did Dale give you a recap at least?"

She shook her head, lips pursed. "Only that it was about you, and he'd been sworn to secrecy beyond that because he'd already said too much. That's how I knew you must've told him you knew about Ava. I waited for you to call. When you didn't, I thought about going over to your house or calling you. Eventually, I thought you might just need time to process."

"I did," I said. "Thank you."

"Have you spoken to him today?"

"Not really. He drove me home this morning without speaking or looking at me more than absolutely necessary."

Cami frowned. "This morning?"

I felt the heat rising over my cheeks as I remembered a small detail I hadn't mentioned. "He asked me to stay at his place last night after a little scare with my firepit."

Her brows rose high beneath her side-swept bangs. "It sounds like we have a lot more to talk about than I realized."

"Probably." I laughed. "It's been a wild few days. That's for sure."

"This is going to be okay," she promised. "Mason will come around."

I shrugged. "It's fine if it's not," I said, hating the lie in the words, even as I spoke them. "I like Mason. I'm attracted to Mason. I trust and respect Mason. But I'm not in the market for complicated friendships right now, and I'm definitely not looking for anything romantic. I mean, I'd have to be crazy to walk through that fire again. I've already been thoroughly burned."

She frowned. "Your ex and my ex were rotten, awful men. But they were exceptions. They were not the rule."

I took shallow sips of cool air, mooring myself against the torrent of feelings. "When he walked out last night," I said, voice falling and stomach coiling, "it felt the same way it did every time Grant walked away. No explanation. No conversation. Just me being left behind. Like I wasn't important enough to spare a few words, to fight for, or with. I don't want that in my life ever again. Not from anyone."

Her expression turned to heartbreak, and I looked away to control the brewing tears.

Thankfully, her phone dinged, and she pulled it out, raising a finger. "I am so sorry. It's a vendor."

I pulled in a deep, steadying breath and scanned the scene, looking for a distraction. I returned smiles and waves as Cami texted frantically behind me.

"All done," she said a moment later. "Why don't you come over for dinner at my place tonight?" She tucked her phone out of sight. "Food. Wine. Talking. It's been too long since we've done all of that at one time."

I smiled, slightly reinflated by the image she'd painted. "What about Dale? I don't want to be a third wheel."

"You won't."

"Where will he be?" I asked. "Is he leaving again?" Maybe the wine and girl talk were as much for her as for me.

Her lips quirked, fighting a delighted smile. "He's looking for a house here."

"What?" I rose onto my toes and hugged her. "Cami, that's amazing."

She squealed quietly. "I think he's really the one," she said.

"I don't know what kind of magic Gretchen works over there at Golden Matches, but she knows love. She saw him coming. She knew."

I hugged her again, not believing for a minute that anyone, even sweet, mystical Gretchen, could tell someone when they'd meet their soul mate. I wasn't even sure I believed in soul mates. But I was thrilled for Cami.

"He can work from anywhere," she went on. "His work with the FBI is done virtually more often than not, anyway."

"I'm so happy for you both," I said. My heart swelled, seeming to absorb the joy radiating from her skin. "I'll be there after work, and I will bring the dessert."

"It's a date!"

I slipped out of work a little early when Lexi offered to close up. A ladies' night with Cami sounded like exactly the balm my heart and nerves needed. And once she got past the fact that I'd been threatened once or twice this week, I was sure she'd help me decide what to do next.

Clyde and I slipped into the lake house quietly, then turned on all the lights. I checked under the beds and in the closets for killers while he waited at his food bowl, in a true show of teamwork.

"We're alone," I told him, returning to the tune of his hunger yowls.

He curled around my feet as I cracked the lid on a can of wet food, feeling entirely too lazy to boil and shred chicken.

"Cami invited me for dinner," I explained, scooping the can's contents onto a paper plate and serving it to the Lord of the castle. "I'll be gone a few hours, and I need you to tell me if anyone comes over while I'm away. Can you do that? Maybe get a description if you don't recognize them."

Clyde concentrated on his meal while I went to change clothes.

"What do you think?" I asked a few minutes later, when he appeared in my bedroom doorway.

I'd selected dark leggings, fuzzy socks and an ugly sweater with an embroidered cartoon turkey. The words, Ready to Get Stuffed, ran under the bird's orange feet. The ensemble seemed appropriate for an evening of comfort food and wine. I could easily eat my feelings and hide the resulting bloat. A complete win-win.

Clyde licked his chops, then his paw to wash his face.

I glanced in the mirror, debating my makeup and hair situation. Given the outfit, I decided to spend a minute refreshing the lipstick and mascara. My hair was the same whether I tried to wrangle it or not, so I went with *not* and grabbed a jacket on my way out the door.

The drive to Cami's was uneventful, so I used the time to mentally rehash everything I knew about Mr. Fryer, his death and his relationships while alive. Tom from the Road Crew and Vivian from Gnome Alone both had financial reasons to confront him. Alyssa, his neighbor, had grounds for a beef too. Actually, in that case, Fryer had the reason for complaint. Regardless, it wasn't hard to imagine a situation where the two neighbors might've had an altercation that went south.

Then there was Jean, the woman, who'd helped herself to his store for no clear reason I could see. To hang a sign?

Not to think ill of the dead, but Fryer's social circle, as far as I could see, was a dumpster fire. If I was murdered, and someone had to interview my friends and family, the person asking questions would quickly see that I was loved, respected and lucky to have the people I did in my life. What the fictional detective would not find was a bunch of folks who all had reason to want to hurt me.

I slowed as Cami's dramatic black-and-white colonial came into view. Solar lights and flowerbeds lined the drive and walkway to her magazine-worthy porch. Red rocking chairs flanked her porch swing, and a happy scarecrow welcomed visitors. Battery-operated candles flickered in every window.

I grabbed my purse and bakery box, then marched up the flagstone path with enthusiasm.

The door sucked open before I could knock.

"Come in," Cami sang, pulling me into the foyer and wrapping me in a hug. "I'm so glad you're here. I feel like a terrible friend. You've been dealing with so much, and I've been busy with Dale and the Makers Market prep. It's time we caught up."

I stepped out of her embrace and passed her the box. "My mama's hummingbird cake."

Her mouth opened. "This is my absolute favorite of your family recipes. My mama's favorite too, so you know I'm going to have to save her a piece somehow."

"Good luck," I said. "I wore my stretchy pants."

Hummingbird cake originated in Jamaica and was named after the national bird. Southerners got hooked on the multi-layered cinnamon, banana, pineapple and pecan recipe before I was born, and a few Blissers tried to master their own versions of the original. Mama's was the best.

I followed Cami through her open-concept family area to the island bar in the kitchen, peeling off my jacket as I moved. The delectable scents of dinner in her oven made my mouth water. Biscuits, ham, gravy and potatoes. It had been far too long since I'd had a proper homecooked dinner. I hung my jacket on the back of one tall island chair with an appreciative *Mmm*.

She set the cake near her wine rack, then upturned two

glasses. "White or red?" Her expression soured before I could answer, so I waited. "What are you wearing?"

I looked at my casual, if silly, outfit, then back at Cami. "Comfy clothes. Warm and stretchy."

Her simple black dress was fitted and accompanied by a double-string of pearls.

"What are you wearing?" I asked. "I thought this was a ladies' night. I came to overeat and complain."

Her eyelids closed slowly.

"Is someone else coming?" I asked, looking around. "I didn't see Dale's car in the drive."

"He went to pick up some things," she said, peeling her lids open once more.

I smiled. "I don't care if Dale sees me looking silly. This sweater makes me smile, and I really do plan to get stuffed."

She covered her mouth with one hand and snorted.

"You're right," she said, pouring herself a glass of red wine. "Tell me everything."

"Thank you." I pointed to the other bottle, and she poured me a glass of white wine.

We stood in the kitchen, drinking and snacking on a platter of olives, cheese chunks and assorted crackers, while I unloaded every crazy detail from the past few days, starting with Fryer's passive-aggressive notes in my Gifts of Gratitude box and ending with my chat on the square with Vivian a few hours before.

Cami listened like I was retelling a horror story, frown deepening and eyes widening progressively. She refilled our glasses with a slightly shaky hand, then squeezed my fingers when she set the bottle aside. "I hate that you've been in danger and I didn't know. You can tell me anything," she insisted. "You know that. It doesn't matter if Dale's in town or if you know I'm going to tell you to knock it off and be safe. You still need to tell me. I want to know. It's what best friends are for."

"I appreciate that," I said. "Finishing the lake house and helping Gigi prepare to buy the Blissful Bean space was keeping me plenty busy after work. Then Fryer died, and things got dicey pretty fast, but I'm really glad you invited me over tonight. I needed this."

"Me too," she said warmly. "I just wish you hadn't worn that shirt."

A male voice carried through her back door, then the doorknob turned.

Dale walked inside with a six pack of beers from the Great Lakes Brewing Company in one hand, and Mason on his heels.

"Oh. My. Lord," I whispered-screeched to Cami. "Are you kidding me?"

"Surprise," she whispered back.

Mason's gaze landed on me and he grimaced. His eyes moved lower, scanning my sweater, and his lips twitched.

"Oh, look," Dale said. "Bonnie's here." His smile was comically wide and obviously a result of overacting. "We took the alley and parked out back. Didn't even notice a car out front."

"Did ya now?" I asked flatly, sliding my eyes to Cami.

She beamed and raised the bottle of wine. "Refill?"

CHAPTER SIXTEEN

*A*n hour later, the meal had been eaten in palpable tension, and the four of us had moved to the living room, where we sat in more awkward silence, exchanging uncomfortable glances. I hadn't even been able to overeat like I'd planned with everyone looking at me. And I'd passed on the hummingbird cake. But at least I'd saved lots of room for wine.

When I reached the bottom of my third glass, I cracked.

"What?" I said, moving my attention from Dale to Cami, then back. "Just say it. This night has been rough enough without the two of you doing whatever it is you're doing."

Cami gave her head a small nod and narrowed her eyes meaningfully at Dale.

He clasped his hands and nodded at me. "I think it's time we address the elephant in the room."

"Here we go," Mason groaned.

I glared. "Rude."

Dale cocked his head. "We all know the two of you are fighting. We all know why. And we all want it to end. So, why can't we all discuss it? Settle it. Fix it."

Cami patted Dale's shoulder, then went to open a new bottle of wine.

Mason worked his jaw, cheeks darkening. "This is none of your business. And it's not something we all need to discuss. Ever." His voice was hard and thick with meaning as he stared at his friend. "In fact, it wasn't something one of us should ever have opened his mouth about to start with."

"I was trying to—"

Mason raised a hand. "I've heard it, and I don't care. It wasn't your story to tell."

Cami shot a pleading look in my direction, as if my problem with Mason hurt her somehow.

"We all care about one another," Dale argued. "So it is our business. You might not like that, Mr. Lone Ranger, but we're a team." He circled a finger overhead, as if indicating the four of us in the room. "Me and you. You and Bonnie. Me and Cami. Cami and Bonnie. And it's a team worth being on. One worth mending when it's hurt."

I smiled. Maybe it was the wine, but I didn't hate the thought of being on a team like this one, especially if Gigi could join.

Mason rolled his shoulders and tipped the glass of water in his hand toward Dale. He hadn't had anything else to drink since he'd walked through the door. "Bonnie and I aren't fighting."

"Well, you aren't speaking," Dale challenged. "At least, not in the hour or so since you got here."

Mason glanced at me, and I looked away, hating the ambush as much as he was. "We aren't not speaking," he said.

Dale lifted his beer in mock acceptance. "Great. What's new?"

"My buddy's moving to Bliss," Mason said, looking my way once more. "You might know him. He's the one with the big mouth."

Cami gasped. She set the new bottle of wine on the coffee table near our glasses. "I think you meant to say the one who cares so much about you."

"No." Mason shook his head. "I got it right the first time."

Dale sucked his teeth, unaffected.

I squirmed and refilled my glass for the third...fourth time? "How's the murder investigation going?" I asked, my voice a little funny. "Any leads on who hurt Mr. Fryer?"

Mason turned his grouchy face in my direction. "You mean anything besides the apology note left at the scene? By you?"

"Yes."

Cami wiggled onto the overstuffed armchair with Dale and whispered something that sounded a lot like "uh oh."

I blinked slowly, feathers effectively ruffled. "You know I did not kill Mr. Fryer," I said, speaking each word slowly and with bite. The wine had warmed my body from the inside out, and I liked it. Grant never let me drink more than one glass at a dinner party. One was polite. Two said I was a lush.

A small snort bubbled out as I wondered what Mr. Rules would think of me now. In my Get Stuffed turkey shirt on my third-ish glass of wine. "Ha," I said to no one in particular.

Mason frowned. His eyes flashed in challenge, and I stood, leaving my glass on the coffee table. He rose with me.

We were going to fight.

And everything began to bing bong inside me like Fourth of July fireworks. I didn't have to watch what I said anymore. Not in this house, or mine, or anywhere. I could be blunt and forthright. And I could be mad.

"You invited me over last night," I said. "Insisted I come, for my protection. Then you offered me a drink and leaned in like you were about to say something life altering, but instead you ran off after I told you what I knew about your past."

He set his hands on his hips, looking like I was the one who was in the wrong. "You couldn't have told me that before I got up the nerve to tell you…"

"Tell me what?" I snapped, stepping in his direction. I lifted my chin and squared my shoulders. "Because if you can't handle my curiosity, my questions and opinions and the occasional blurted confession, then maybe you need to rethink whatever it is you planned to say."

"You don't think I do?" he groused. "Only every day of my life."

Beside us, Cami gasped. "Did he just…"

Dale shushed her.

I narrowed my eyes, hoping I was standing tall and not waving slightly back and forth as I suspected. "I told you the truth later than I should have, but I will always tell you the truth. I'm out of practice right now, after walking on egg shells most of my adult life, but I'm game to improve if you can stop running off!" My voice rose an octave and cracked a little. "Sorry. I feel carried away."

"She might need to be carried away," Dale whispered. "How much wine did you feed her?"

Cami laughed and hit his chest with her perfectly mani-cured hand.

I should get manicured more often.

"You can tell me anything," Mason shouted back.

My face snapped around in his direction. "Good!"

"Great!"

We stared at one another, and my heart pounded in my ears.

"You shouldn't have run off," I said. "You left me alone after telling me you were going to protect me, and I'm mad. I count on you for things."

He dipped his chin and flicked his eyes toward our friends, then back. "I know. I won't leave you like that again."

"How can I know?" I asked. My hands rose at my sides, desperate for some way to know he could be counted on if things got tough again.

"You can't know," he snapped. "I'm going try to do better. And you have to hang around and let me."

I frowned. "Fine."

His brows rose, and his expression morphed to confusion. "Fine?"

"Yeah."

"You want to get out of here?" he asked.

I grabbed my coat from the chair by the island.

Mason opened the back door and ushered me out. "Thanks for dinner, Cami," he called over his shoulder, while I waved. "Dale," he said. "Tomorrow?"

Dale dipped his chin.

We climbed into Mason's Jeep, parked behind Dale's truck.

"You didn't ride with Dale?" I asked, buckling in as we reversed into the alley.

"Nope. I never know when I've got to cut and leave," he said.

He meant for sheriff business, but I smiled anyway, thankful his Jeep had been an available getaway car.

We rode through the night in a strange, electrified silence, stealing looks at one another as we passed beneath streetlights.

"I don't mean to make you crazy," I said. "I make myself nuts too. I think it's a personality defect."

Mason frowned. "You don't have a personality defect."

"But I do make you crazy."

He grinned. "You have a way of getting under my skin."

"Why is that, I wonder?"

"Why indeed," he said.

When the lake came into view, shrouded in night and shadows from clustered trees, he pulled the Jeep off the road and shifted into park.

I stared at the moonlight rippling over the water, then looked carefully at the man beside me. I admired the little crow's feet at the corners of his eyes, hard-earned from all the glaring and laughing he did. I liked the flecks of gray through his hair and the square line of his jaw. I really liked the package he had going on from the chin down as well, but mostly, I liked everything I couldn't see but knew was there. His strength. His smarts. The pride he took in his work. And most of all, the hero's heart that beat just beneath the surface of a whole lot of pain.

Mason Wright was a salty hard-shelled peanut with a warm marshmallow center.

I was pretty sure I'd been trapped in that center since the day he'd first revealed it to me.

"What are you thinking about?" he asked, sliding his hands along the steering wheel and turning his eyes my way.

"Marshmallows."

"Of course." He opened his door and climbed out. "You want to walk?"

"Yeah." I met him at the Jeep's grill, then accepted his outstretched hand.

He released me when I was steady, but I used his crooked arm as a guide in the darkness.

We walked along the water's edge, listening to the lapping water, the singing crickets and croaking frogs. The darkness was enveloping. The millions of stars, mesmerizing.

Brisk, clean air rushed through my lungs as we moved, clearing my head of the wine buzz and replacing that with another kind of intoxication all together.

Mason set his hand over mine, where it rested on his arm.

"I never expected to stay here," he said. "I only agreed to come and see what small-town life was about because it served double duty. We had leads that Devon Grimes— Zander," he clarified, "was in the area. I wanted to find him, and Cleveland PD wanted me to take some time off after my undercover stint. The chief worried about the impact Ava's death had on me."

I drifted at his side, interested in his words. Eager to hear anything he wanted to share.

"I thought I'd come down here, look into a few leads, sniff around for signs of Grimes, then tell the chief I was recuperated and ready for my next assignment. I did a few mandated counseling sessions online. Telehealth," he said. "I think I exhausted the poor sap in charge of deeming me well, but he signed the papers, so I was free to return to the job."

"But you didn't," I said.

"No, I didn't."

"Couldn't pass up an opportunity to guard a quirky little town?"

He smiled, eyes fixed to the horizon. "That was partly it. This place is a little surreal. Like living in a storybook. With murders. It's just about as different from Cleveland as I could've imagined. Probably exactly what I'd needed. I hated it at first."

I frowned. "No one hates Bliss."

"Well, I didn't love it," he said, casting me a quick look. "It's weird here. Everyone's always smiling and waving and lifting their chin in recognition when you drive by or make eye contact, even if you've never seen the person before in your life. I've got sixteen casseroles in my freezer. Women bring them to the sheriff's department. I can't bring myself to throw them out, so I'm either going to have to throw a party or buy a second freezer. And I don't throw parties. Also, I swear I sneezed at the town square yesterday and thirty-seven people blessed me."

I smiled. "I think you like our little hamlet."

He laughed, head shaking. "It's been an unexpected journey. That's for certain."

I caught his eye, and the smoldering look I found there curled my toes inside my sneakers.

"I'm also experiencing a lot of...feelings."

"Feelings?" I asked, nose wrinkled. "You didn't have feelings before you moved here?"

"No." He grimaced. "Lawmen don't have feelings. We have other things. Better things, like clarity of thought, instinct and action."

"What about Ava?" I asked. "You were undercover when you became involved with her, which means you were technically on duty all the time. Being a lawman didn't stop you then."

"This is different," he said, peeking down at me again. "What I had with Ava was complicated, and it revolved around a crime syndicate. Our relationship was tainted. We were bound by mutual fear. Me of being found out, and her of being deemed disposable."

My heart broke for him and for Ava, who had, in the end, been deemed disposable. "I'm sorry."

He waved me off. "I came here to satisfy the demands of my shrink and my captain," he went on. "I was supposed to be dealing with what had happened with Ava. Five minutes later, I met you, and I thought to myself, this is not good."

"You thought I killed an old lady for her ball gowns."

"You looked so small in that big house and fancy dining room, all curled into yourself, hugging a crate with a cat in it, like he was your life raft."

"He usually is," I said. "Clyde and I have been through a lot."

Mason stopped moving and turned to face me. "See, that's the problem. From that very first minute, I hated that you were alone. I was still mad at you for making me spill my coffee earlier, when you almost ran me over, but there was just something about you. There is something about you," he corrected. "I want to be your life raft."

I forced my eyes to meet his, reminding myself I was brave and strong, and Mason wouldn't judge or belittle me. "You do?"

His tall, lean body grew still and cautious. His sharp blue eyes flashed in the night. "Are you sure you want to talk about this?" he asked. "Because sometimes I get the idea you do, and other times, I think there's no way you're ready. I've got plenty to say, but I'm not here to make you uncomfortable. And I can't read your mind, so you're going to have to be the one to set the pace."

I swallowed hard, recognizing his hesitation as a gift. He'd offered me a way out before we got in any deeper.

We'd talked a lot over the months since we'd met. And he knew I had things of my own to work on. Like the fact that I ripped the size tags out of my clothes because no amount of self-love and feminism could seem to make me not care about the numbers my ex-husband had checked diligently since I was nineteen. He knew I gave myself whispered pep talks when I got frazzled and nervous, sometimes unintentionally and aloud.

I knew he hated sweet tea, because he was a city slicker, a northerner, and therefore clueless about a great number of things. And he hated chickens. He compared them to feathery aliens and called them unnatural when I mentioned the popular new trend of keeping several in your yard like pets.

"Bonnie," he whispered, inhaling long and slow as he waited for my answer.

Aside from Cami, Mason was my closest friend, and I'd only known him a few months. I trusted him, and I didn't trust easily. That was something. He knew what I'd been through, and that I was broken in a lot of places.

He raised large, warm hands to cup my jaw.

A rush of unexpected tears blurred my eyes. "I'm not ready."

Mason dipped his chin in acceptance, expression unchanged. Then he removed his hands from my face and said, "Let's just enjoy the walk."

CHAPTER SEVENTEEN

J had breakfast with my family the next morning. Clyde prowled the fields of wildflowers alongside the barn cats, while Gigi, my folks and I drank coffee and ate French toast on the patio.

My folks were dressed for work, in their usual attire. Dad in work pants and a logoed T-shirt. Mom in a matching T-shirt, a dozen sizes smaller, and denim overalls, one strap perpetually falling from her narrow shoulders.

I sat beside Dad and across the table from two older versions of me. The similarities in our appearances were borderline creepy. Like looking into a magic mirror that revealed how I would age. My hair would get slowly shorter. My skin impossibly paler and significantly looser. My mouth infinitely bigger.

I smiled.

"And you said what?" Mama asked her mother. She shoveled berries onto her toast, pride and shock racing over her pretty face.

"You know it," Gigi said. "I agreed to sell the man's coffees at my bakery. That's worth something."

"And he just knocked the price down by ten thousand dollars?"

Gigi sat taller and lifted her steaming mug with comic slowness. Then grinned over the rim. "Yep."

I couldn't believe it. "You got Dave to knock ten grand off the sale price?"

She nodded.

"That will pay for all your renovations," I said.

"Yep."

Dad stretched back on his chair. "Impressive, Gigi."

"Thank you," she said. "You don't get to be this old without learning how to spin a few things to your benefit. He'll get the ten grand back in coffee sales within a year. Meanwhile, I can upgrade a few things with that savings. The rest will go into a rainy day fund, in case something unexpected comes up."

Mom squeezed her hand, still marveling.

"They're switching out the shop signs today," Gigi said. "I'm moving the old Blissful Bean sign inside as part of the décor, and putting up a new Oh, My Goodies unit in its place. A white oval with teal letters. Very cute and a little kitschy. Like me."

We laughed, and Mama slung her arm around Gigi. "No doubt."

"I'll put paper over the windows with the words coming soon stenciled through the center," Gigi said, "so folks know we're working on it. I read online that I can build early buzz and anticipation that way." She set her cup aside and caught my eye. "I've already reached out to the crews who helped you with the lake house renovations and offered them the work."

I smiled, delighted by the knowledge my return had resulted in more jobs for local families. "Excellent."

Mama turned happy eyes on me. "We've been meaning to

get out to your place and take a look at the progress. Rumor has it you've outdone yourself. Ladies around town are saying you're an interior design guru."

"Quite a compliment," I said. "No one's been over to visit," except Mason, "and I'm not finished decorating, so I guess the workers are commenting to their wives?"

She tapped her nose, indicating I'd guessed correctly. "And taking photos. Not a lot, and nothing big picture, but everyone's buzzing about your palette, flooring and woodwork."

"Cabinets were installed yesterday," I said. "They're perfect." Workers had tried to save the originals, but the damage was too severe, so I'd selected something new. I'd admired the completed kitchen last night after Mason dropped me off. Cami and Dale had already delivered my car to the driveway. Apparently, I'd forgotten my purse and keys in my haste to leave with Mason.

"I can't wait to see," Mama said.

"The décor is all from my store," I told her. "I thought it'd be a great way to stand by my product and show folks I love the things I sell."

"This is exactly what I wanted to hear." Mama looked to Gigi. "I'll put together the housewarming party."

Gigi raised a triumphant finger. "Put me down for desserts."

I frowned. "My home isn't big enough to host a party. The property is nice, but it's getting cooler outside all the time. A cookout won't work either."

Mama and Gigi didn't look up from their phones, reading glasses had appeared on their noses.

"Too late now," Dad said under his breath. "It's best to just get on board. Arguing will only waste time and get everyone worked up. But it won't stop the party."

I tipped my head against his shoulder, smiling at the perfection of the moment. "Don't I know it."

Lexi was behind the counter at Bless Her Heart when I arrived. She'd opened on time and set up the sidewalk display.

"Nice work," I told her, pausing to free Clyde from his carrier before tucking my purse behind the counter. "The displays are fantastic."

"Thanks," she said, moving to the window, where she could string more words of gratitude. "I took a lot of art classes in high school. I can't draw or paint, but I know what looks good and what doesn't. You'd sold most of what was outside yesterday, so I made do with what I found in here along the same lines."

She finished and joined me at the register. "You look great."

I smiled. "Thanks." I'd worn a royal-blue sweater dress with wide black belt and tall dress boots. My hair was twisted into a messy bun, and I'd wrapped a wide black band around my head to keep the falling pieces away from my eyes.

She'd donned a pair of skinny jeans with tan suede booties and a long cream off-the-shoulder top.

"You look a little like a Pinterest pin yourself," I said.

Lexi lifted one shoulder and batted her eyes. "I'm learning from the best. By the way, I hear your date went well."

I turned slowly to face her. "What?"

She smirked. "My best friend, Kate, saw your car and the HANS's Jeep outside Cami Swartz's place last night, and everyone knows her boyfriend is in town right now because those two are attached at the lips. Kate figured the four of you were having a double date, even though you parked out front and he parked out back. If that was supposed to throw off the gossips, it totally didn't work."

I gaped, then pulled myself together, oddly thankful for the distinct lack of shoppers. "Dale and Mason know one another from Cleveland," I said. "They were friends before either of them came here."

"Sure, but that doesn't explain why the four of you were at Ms. Swartz's place at the same time," she said. "At night. If not for dinner."

"It was for dinner," I said, flummoxed and knowing the more I protested, the guiltier I looked. Not that there was any reason to feel guilty. Or to protest. Except that it hadn't been a date. "It wasn't a date," I repeated.

"If you say so," Lexi said. "You still look cute today, and I hear the lake house is looking great too."

"It is," I agreed, winding my way through the store to expend a sudden burst of energy. "Should I ask where you heard that?"

"My neighbor's sister dates one of the guys on the electrical crew. He took some pictures of the light fixtures when he finished the installation. He was discreet, but there's no denying it looks fantastic. He hopes the photos of his work will help him get more jobs in the future."

I nodded. "Tell him I'm happy to write letters of recommendation or make as many phone calls as he needs."

I'd told each crew member the same thing before they finished their jobs, but it never hurt to tell them all again.

"That's real kind," she said. "There aren't a lot of opportunities for electricians right now. Some get lucky and find jobs outside town, but most are doing farm work until someone needs them for electrical again."

I smiled, knowing Gigi had more jobs on the way.

"I don't mind the workers sharing sneak peeks at the interior. I plan to display some of the final photos at the shop when everything is done. Plus, Mama and Gigi are planning a housewarming, so half the town will probably take a spin through the place soon."

Lexi clapped her hands silently. "Don't you just love that? Knowing so many people around town and feeling like we're all just one big team or something? I can't decide what I want to do with my life, but I definitely don't want to leave town. Not even for college."

"Have you thought about the community college in Cromwell?" I asked.

Bliss was superior in many ways, but we didn't have an establishment of higher education.

Lexi let her jaw fall open. "Ms. Balfour. Did you just say the C word?"

"I'm just asking," I said, smiling as she teased.

Lexi thought it over for a minute. "My old babysitter lives there. She's pretty cool. Mama said she's opening a soufflé stand soon. She asked me to help her however I could."

My thoughts ran immediately to the woman I'd met while in line for coffee. "Does your friend carry a chicken in a pet crate?"

"How do you know that?" Lexi asked. "Did she stop in here and I missed her?"

"No, I was in line behind her recently at Blissful Bean." My thoughts were cut short by the sight of a pickup parade.

"What is going on out there?" Lexi asked, moving to the window for a closer look.

Maybe parade wasn't the right word, I decided, joining Lexi at the glass. There weren't any majorettes or marching bands, but there was a definite caravan of sorts. A somber, silent procession of old trucks flying black flags. Men with dark armbands, their elbows hung over the open windows looking as if they were headed to a funeral.

The trucks parked outside The Truck Stop, drawing onlookers from all around.

I opened the door and held it while Lexi followed me onto the sidewalk.

Silence loomed over the square.

Beautiful oak trees in a blaze of fall colors partially obstructed my view, but the trucks and dismounting drivers were easy to discern. The members of the caravan stood before their vehicles, hands clasped behind them, before marching up the single step and into The Truck Stop.

"What are they doing?" Lexi whispered.

Slowly, the frozen shoppers and pedestrians churned into motion once more.

I stared at the parked trucks. "Fryer is dead," I said. "He had no wife, no ex-wife and no children. No business partner either. And from what I've gathered, no truly close friends. Just a self-proclaimed truck-club groupie, who memorized the key code to get into his shop, and has used it on more than one occasion since his death. Apparently to invite the whole club over today."

I couldn't even understand why the Road Crew would be there. None of them had seemed particularly upset by his passing, and Tom had seemed to loathe him.

"Super creepyville," Lexi said.

I didn't disagree.

"Are you going over there again?" she asked. "Find out what they're up to? Some kind of wake?"

I considered it a moment, then reminded myself Jean would definitely be there, and she knew my name wasn't Dharma. "No. Not this time."

But maybe I could ask Gretchen to sweep her sidewalk outside Golden Matches. She'd have an excellent view from there, and she could report back.

The back doorbell buzzed.

Lexi and I jumped, then laughed.

She dragged a hand through her long hair. "I've got it."

I'd spread the word over time that anyone could leave things anonymously to be considered for my store. They just had to press the bell and be on their way. I'd bring the items in for evaluation and make sure nothing went to waste. Folks took me up on the offer more often than I'd expected.

As it turned out, Blissers seemed to love the fact that they could deliver heirlooms and family hand-me-downs to me guilt free, knowing I would restore them and find them new homes. The bell rang at least once a week, and it was never for a single purse or pair of shoes. It was always an entire closet full of outdated designer clothing, crates of mismatched, but high-quality, China, and gorgeous one-off furniture pieces the owner had no idea what else to do with.

I kept the things I could update to sell, and the rest went to local charities and women's shelters. Nothing was ever wasted.

"I'll come with," I said, knowing most of our donations took several trips and more than two hands.

My phone rang before I reached the rear hallway. "Gretchen's calling."

Lexi smiled. "Tell her I said hi!"

"Hey, Gretchen," I answered, feeling the questions pile on my tongue.

She sighed dramatically in response. "Thank goodness. I wasn't sure you'd answer. I worried you might be on your way to The Truck Stop....You're not, are you?"

"Nope. What's going on over there, anyway?" I asked. "Lexi and I watched a bunch of pickups roll in and park, but we don't have a clear view from here. I almost called you to ask what you could see."

"I know," she said. "It's why I called. They're having a party."

Lexi returned from the back door with a box of high heels and petticoats in her arms. A pair of candelabras dangled from her fingertips, and a confused expression marred her face.

"Let me put you on speaker," I told Gretchen. "It's just us. No shoppers." I pressed the correct option on my screen and extended the phone between us. "Okay. Tell us what you see."

"Some lady put a sign in the window that says private party," Gretchen reported. "They're playing old rock music and getting a little loud. Here comes another truck," she said. "Oh, someone brought pizzas and chips."

My stomach growled unnecessarily, and I mentally told it to get a grip.

Sleighbells jingled against the shop's front door, and I jerked around to see who'd arrived.

Mirabelle dragged herself to the refreshments stand and shoved a cookie in her mouth.

"Gotta go," I said, disengaging the speaker option before pressing the phone to my ear. "Mirabelle's here. Keep me posted."

"You too!" Gretchen said. "Be careful out there, and report back. I'm interested!"

I promised, and we disconnected.

Lexi set the donation box aside and made a run for Mr. Dinky at Mirabelle's side.

She dropped to the floor to rub his head and tummy, talking baby talk while he basked in her affection.

I smiled, missing the days I could drop to the floor like that, knowing nothing would creak or crack as I got back up.

"Hello," I said to Mirabelle. "How's your morning?"

She shot me a no-nonsense look. "I want to know how you have time to do all the things you do."

I waited, not caring for her tone, and suspecting she was in a mood.

"Between remodeling the lake house, running your own store and canoodling with the HANS, I wouldn't think you'd have time to mess with a murder investigation."

Lexi popped up, mouth open. "There was canoodling?"

"No," I said, as Mirabelle declared, "Yes."

Lexi began to bounce. "Every woman in town is waiting on pins and needles for those Good Luck Falls calendars to come in. What is taking them so long?"

Mason and some other men had been photographed earlier this year for an annual fundraiser in the form of a calendar. The men were shirtless and horribly objectified near a waterfall locals believed was good luck.

I'd ordered two. One for work and one for home.

"Any day now," Mirabelle said. "They're always in before Thanksgiving."

Lexi clapped.

"How do you know I'm digging into the investigation?" I asked, bringing us back to the more important topic at hand.

"Please," Mirabelle said. "Everyone knows. I need to write a follow-up piece on Fryer's death, and no new police reports have been filed, which means I'd have to dig up some dirt on my own, and I don't want to. So, what can you give me?"

I bit my lip. "Did you know there's a party at The Truck Stop?" I asked.

She nodded. "Sure. It's Fryer's wake. Some lady called the paper to have it covered in the local section. My editor says it's crime adjacent and that means I have to cover that too. I'm heading over there next."

"The whole wake is a crime," I said, explaining how Jean had no claim to the property or any business entering it. Never mind throwing a party there or asking to have the bash covered in the *Bliss Bugle*. It was beginning to seem as if she'd do anything for attention.

Mirabelle opened her purse and rolled a bright-green

stick of gum into her mouth. Her gaze lifted to the window, presumably thinking about the party across the square. "I guess it's time for me to see what the folks at The Truck Stop know. Walk with me," she said. "Mr. Dinky has to tinkle. He had a lot of water at our last stop, and his bladder isn't as young as it used to be. You can hold his leash, then bring him back here for a bit while I work. You don't mind, do you?"

I looked from Mirabelle to Mr. Dinky, suddenly concerned about his aged bladder and the freshly steamed rug he'd curled on. "Okay, but I can't attend the wake. I need to get back."

Mirabelle shrugged, and I took the dog's leash.

"I can't believe I'm covering a wake for that old curmudgeon," she complained. "I'm tired. I want a break. We need some fresh blood on this paper. At the rate I'm going, I could live to one hundred and never retire."

I patted her shoulder. The navy *Bliss Bugle* windbreaker was slick under my touch.

"If these people don't belong here, someone should call the HANS," she said.

"Not me," I said, determined not to interact with Mason about this case any more than absolutely necessary. Things were complicated enough between us already, and he got all prickly whenever I asked about his investigations. "It's none of my business."

"Like that's ever stopped you."

True. "Any thoughts on who killed Fryer? There might not be any new police reports, but is your gut telling you anything about this case?"

"I don't listen to my gut. I follow facts," she said flatly, easily. As if she hadn't given the matter any consideration at all. "And so far the facts are few and far between. Why? What does your gut say?"

I told her more about Jean the groupie, then Tom, AKA

Axel, and how he felt lowballed over the sale of his truck. Then I reported what Vivian said about the sale of Gnome Alone, supporting Tom's lowball claim, and her opinion on Alyssa, Fryer's neighbor. "It's like he had no problem taking advantage of people. The lowball accusation isn't exactly a smoking gun, but it's interesting. Right?"

She stopped on the sidewalk and turned her back to The Truck Stop. "Yes. Here's what I have. Also not a big red bullseye, but like you said, *interesting*."

I waited on pins and needles for her next words, while she effected a dramatic pause.

"I found two recently filed police reports over a conflict between Fryer and his neighbor. Apparently they'd fight, and it'd get heated. So, the deputies would go out. It's been too long since the boundaries were properly surveyed, so the deputies just defused the conflict and told the pair to work things out in court." She raised her brows, as if to say, how do you like them apples. "I can't print any of that, of course, because it's not directly relevant to the case until the sheriff's department says it is. And it makes Alyssa look like a suspect. I had no plans to follow up on the potential lead because I'm not an investigator, but it sounds like you're already on it."

I pressed my lips tight, suppressing the urge to claim I wasn't on it. Also wondering if it might've killed Mirabelle to extend the same courtesy to Gigi last summer, or me the spring before, when she'd had no problem printing things that implied our guilt. Instead, I focused on another takeaway.

"I need to remember police reports are public record," I said. "My biggest research move so far is Facebook."

She snorted.

"What?" I said. "I'm learning."

The door opened, and we gasped in unison.

I stumbled back a step, having been startled one too many times this year, and thinking again about a therapist.

Jean looked down the steps at us from her place just inside the open door. "What are you doing out there?" she asked, gaze sliding from me to Mirabelle's *Bliss Bugle* jacket. "We've been waiting for you."

Mirabelle climbed the step, and went inside. Jean closed the door behind her, making it clear I wasn't invited.

A relief because I had no intention of explaining why I'd used a fake name the other night, and what I was really up to.

I turned with a sigh, and my gaze caught on Tom inside the shop window, glaring pointedly back.

CHAPTER EIGHTEEN

*G*ray clouds rolled thick and heavy through the sky just before dinner. The party at The Truck Stop was going strong. Not a single pickup had moved in hours, and I couldn't get Tom's angry glare from my mind, no matter how hard I tried.

Mirabelle had collected Mr. Dinky from Lexi when she'd volunteered to take him for another walk on the square, and I'd missed the chance to hear what Mirabelle had learned. I planned to call her tomorrow afternoon if I didn't hear from her first.

The world outside my window was unnaturally dark as I carefully repainted the set of newly donated candelabras. Shoppers hurried from store to store, tipped forward against the driving wind and holding tight to shopping bags, animated by the repeating gusts.

I'd ordered dinner for two, and Lexi had braved the weather to retrieve it.

Somehow being alone in the store with Clyde felt less cozy and more ominous than knowing she was out alone in the brewing storm.

A fat drop of rain hit the window with a plink, catching Clyde's attention as it slid slowly down.

He set his paw on the large white button he'd been playing hockey with across my floor, then chattered at the raindrop.

"I guess the storm's here," I said, abandoning the candelabra in favor of saving my sidewalk display.

I pushed the door open and wind raked it from my grasp, smacking it hard against the wall at one side. "Goodness!" My hair blew across my face, stinging my eyes and temporarily blinding me as I shoved the door closed and went to work, collecting my outdoor items. I piled everything onto the wagon and tugged it gingerly toward the door.

Around me, shopkeeps rushed to dismantle and save their displays while little mobs of fallen leaves lifted into tiny twisters, following the occasional flyer and plastic bag across the street.

Awnings flapped. Lightning flashed.

And in the distance, thunder rolled.

I stared at the ominous world outside as I secured myself back behind the safety of my shop door. The beautiful hanging flower baskets I admired by day rocked wildly from lampposts in the brooding, gloomy night. Something about the combination of fall décor, seasonal darkness and the brewing storm sent shivers down my spine and goosebumps across my skin.

The ongoing wake for a recently murdered shop owner across the square didn't help.

I'd done my best not to think about it, and spent some time with shoppers before selecting the candelabras as my new painting project.

I'd sanded away the bits of dirt and rust, letting my mind wander and asking myself what the candelabras should be in their new lives. Shiny black? Matte? Metallic silver or gold? I'd quickly moved on to white, pale green or navy blue, and saw them seated on my mantle, hearth or dining room table. Accented by the repurposed lantern I'd purchased from the yard sale.

My selfishness had won out, and I'd resolved to make the donations my own. Another home might've benefited from their beauty, but the lake house was a project I couldn't seem to quit.

Clyde made a low, guttural sound, and I froze. He crept toward the window, so low and fast he was little more than a shadow with wide, watching eyes.

The whistle of wind drew my ear toward the back hallway. A small *thunk* followed.

Then another.

Thunk.

Thunk.

Thunk.

Not a knock.

Not footsteps.

Just an unfamiliar, repeated, bumping.

I hefted the heavy goose-head cane I'd uncovered at an estate sale in New Orleans and moved cautiously toward the hall. I considered calling Mason, or running out the front door, but what was there to report? A strange sound? And wasn't it more dangerous in the dark night?

I considered grabbing Clyde and simply going home. No one else would be shopping tonight. Not with the kind of storm we would soon endure.

But what about Lexi? And what was that sound?

Thunk.

Thunk.

Thunk.

Curiosity twisted itself into a tight coil around my lungs

and edged me forward, the cane on one shoulder like a base-ball bat.

I stared down the narrow hall at the back door, eerily outlined in light from the rear lot's lampposts. The deadbolt wasn't set, and wind nudged the door repeatedly in the frame. Just a bit. Only a fraction of an inch. Enough to make the relentless sound.

Thunk. Thunk. Thunk.

I smiled and sighed deeply in relief.

The bells behind me jingled, and the front door crashed open, slamming against the wall once more.

I screamed and spun, cane thrust forward like a sword, elbows locked and knees quaking.

Lexi screamed, and our dinners fell to her feet in multiple logoed take-out bags.

We relaxed at once, laughing and puffing heavy breaths as we scrambled to save our meals.

"Sorry," I repeated, giggling through a bout of nerves as I set the cane aside and moved the food to the counter.

Lexi stripped off her rain-soaked coat. "It was that wind! And the door! Goodness."

A crashing, thunderous *boom* ripped another scream from each of our throats. Both louder and more fervent.

I grabbed the cane as a funnel of icy wind roared into the shop. "The back door."

We hurried to the hall and confirmed. The rattling door had given way, bursting wide and smacking hard against the wall outside.

I blinked at the bright security lighting in the lot. The overall imagery—long dark hallway, bright opening at the end—reminded me of the movie *Poltergeist*, which had scared the cocoa out of me as a child. I needed to close the door before my floor and hall were thoroughly soaked, but I also wondered if I should first tie a rope around my waist and hand the other end to Lexi.

"It's just the wind," I said. "The door was thumping when you came in. I should've secured the deadbolt then, but you dropped the food, and I nearly had a stroke, so..." I smiled awkwardly, heart thrumming hard. "Opening the front door probably created a suction or something, and the back door gave way."

"Right," Lexi said, craning her neck to see around me. "Of course." I took a step into the hallway, and she followed. "Does this remind you of—"

"Don't say it," I said. "It's just the wind. We'll need towels to sop up the rain and dry the wall where it splattered."

"Got it," she said, cutting away for a trip to my office. I'd stored beach towels and summer items in there for the winter.

I picked up my pace as I approached the exit, needing to secure the door.

"It was just the wind," I repeated, willing the words to be true. Then I turned to smile nervously over my shoulder. "I think you forgot to deadbolt the door when you brought the donations in earlier," I said as Lexi caught up, towels over both shoulders and in her hands.

Her eyes were wide as they swept the lot and returned to me. "Maybe," she said. "But I didn't do that."

I followed her horrified gaze to the cracked concrete outside.

Six large white spray-painted letters glowed beneath the rain and lamplight.

WARNED

CHAPTER NINETEEN

en minutes later, Lexi and I sat on the store's large circular checkout counter, legs dangling and take-out containers arranged between us. My appetite had vanished at the sight of the threat, and my limbs were strangely numb, but I was safe, and so were Clyde and Lexi.

Clearly, Clyde had been watching her return with our meals while I'd been focused on the backdoor. Now, Mason was checking the lock and jamb for signs of tampering or forced entry. I supposed it was useless to hope he'd find fingerprints, given the sheeting rain.

Lexi tugged the deep fried folds of her rangoon, revealing its soft cream cheesy center. "Where do you think the HANS was when you called?" she asked. "He got here in like two minutes. He burst in like a hero from a suspense movie, all wet and angry. Ready to save his woman and the day." She dipped part of her rangoon into a cup of sweet-and-sour sauce, then made a show of flexing one arm, muscleman style.

"He was wet because it's raining," I said. "And he's always angry. He was probably picking up his dinner on the square when I called. He always comes around here when he's hungry."

"I'll bet." She wagged her brows. "Why didn't you argue when I said you were his woman?"

I turned one palm up, like that should go without saying. "I'm my own woman. You know that."

"But you want to be his woman."

"Eat your rangoon."

"You guys know I can hear you, right?" Mason called from the hallway. "There's just one thin wall between us." He moved into the archway where we could see him, still wet and grouchy.

Lexi smiled as she shoved the bite between smiling lips. "Any word on the Good Luck Falls calendars? Everyone's waiting."

"No," he said, looking disgruntled. "I still feel duped about my role in that. I can't believe it's a real thing."

"Oh, it's real," Lexi said. "And I've got a feeling they'll raise a record amount this year."

Mason swung his horrified gaze to me.

I forked some fried rice into my mouth. "How's it going back there?"

"The door's secure. No signs of tampering. There's some mild damage to the jamb that was likely caused by the final gust that broke the door loose. If you have a spare key, I'll come back and get that fixed for you."

I nodded. "Absolutely. Thank you."

"Don't mention it." He rubbed a hand over his wet hair, throwing excess water with every swipe. "I haven't found anyone lurking in the closets or corners, so my best guess is that the door opening was a coincidence. Whoever left the note on the parking lot out back probably assumed you'd see it the next time you brought a donation inside."

"Any ideas who left the note?" I asked.

Mason moved to my side, dripping slightly onto the floor and brushing his cool wet clothing against my bare calves. He took my fork, and I shivered at the spark of connection when our fingers touched.

My gaze darted to Lexi, who hadn't missed my short intake of breath. Raising my eyes to Mason's quirked lips revealed that he hadn't missed the little sound either.

He stabbed a piece of my teriyaki chicken and ate it, eyes locked with mine as he chewed. "I have some ideas about who might've left the note," he said a moment later, returning the fork to my hand. "Right now, I'm more interested in what you think."

I glanced at the innocuous plastic utensil, feeling half my age and suddenly fixated on the fact that it had been in his mouth. My ex had refused to touch a cup, bottle or anything else after I had. In hindsight, I could see it was part of his marriage-long campaign to make me feel gross or lesser. One more small, but painful, thread in a much larger tapestry of emotional abuse.

The man before me, however, had no problem putting something into his mouth that had just been in mine. His smile grew as I stared uncontrollably at his lips.

"You're blushing," Lexi said, casually pulling apart another rangoon.

I narrowed my eyes, cheeks heating impossibly further. "Thank you."

She looked toward the storm, still raging outside. "Did you tell him about Jean?"

"I know about Jean," he said.

Lexi made a small grunt, mouth full of fried food. "Did you know she was on the square, at the wake, around the time the message must have been painted. Those letters weren't out there when I brought in the shoes and petticoats."

"She would've also had time to leave the threat in my Gifts of Gratitude box that first night after we spoke and I stopped at Pita Pan," I said.

"And if she's hanging around the square, she would've had access to the tarps in Bonnie's parents' truck," Lexi said.

I twisted on the counter for a better look at her. "You know about the tarps?"

She nodded. "Everyone knows about the tarps."

"Everyone knows about everything around here," Mason grouched. "I'll talk to her again."

"Talk?" I wrinkled my nose. "Aren't you going to arrest her for letting herself into Fryer's store? She doesn't have any right to be there and has absolutely no claim to that space."

He tipped his head back and released a long breath. "She has means to enter without force, and there's no one to say she can't be there. As far as I can tell, she isn't damaging or looting. And I don't mind having people in groups like that." He motioned toward the party across the square. "It's easier to find them."

I rolled my eyes. "Well, as long as it's easier for you."

Mason rested his backside against the counter beside me. "For what it's worth, Jean has an alibi for the night of Fryer's death. She was with one of the other club members. This is not my first rodeo, short stack. So, take it down a notch and let me do my job."

"A short joke?" I asked. "Really? I thought we were past that."

He grinned. "Yeah. I know. But it gets your back up and works as a reliable distraction. How many threats does this make for you now?" He pointed toward the hallway, presumably indicating the message out back.

"This week?" I asked.

He slid his eyes in my direction, and Lexi laughed.

"Have you talked to the guy they call Axel?" I asked. "His

real name is Tom, and he wasn't a fan of Fryer. In fact, he says Fryer was a lowballer. That means he had a habit of taking advantage of folks in tough situations. Like Tom, when he needed to sell his truck to feed his kids, and Vivian from Gnome Alone, when her daughter went to Wharton."

Mason ran a hand over his face before turning to stare at me.

"I'm helping," I said. "Collecting clues. Gathering evidence. It makes your job easier. You just said you liked that."

"It really doesn't." His phone buzzed, and he freed the device from his pocket, exhausted eyes still fixed on me. "Sheriff Wright."

Lexi and I listened while he spoke briefly, and mostly in acronyms, to whoever was on the other end of the line.

He disconnected and put the phone away. "My deputy says no one from The Truck Stop has headed this way in the past few hours."

"How could he know that?" I asked, staring into the darkness once more.

"Stakeout."

"Oh," Lexi said on an exhale. "That's how you got here so fast. You were already nearby spying on the wake."

"I was monitoring the situation," Mason corrected. "I don't spy. Unlike this one." He hooked his thumb in my direction.

I gave the darkness another look. Anyone could go unnoticed out there, especially since the rain had driven everyone inside. And The Truck Stop surely had a back door. "Jean works for her dad," I said, recalling Tom's comment when Jean had arrived at the diner. I wasn't sure if that mattered, or if Mason knew, but I did, and I wanted to make sure he had as many facts as possible.

"I am aware," he said slowly. "They run an auto shop, specializing in classic cars and historic vehicles."

"Oh. That makes a lot of sense."

Headlights flashed over the window as Lexi's phone buzzed. "That's my ride," she said, gathering her things and looking from Mason to me. "Do you need me to do anything else before I go?"

I shook my head. "I think we can take it from here. Be safe out there."

"Back at ya," she said. "Goodnight Sheriff Wright."

Mason lifted a hand, but she didn't look back.

She bounded through the door and into the rain, arms outstretched as if to soak up as many drops as possible, then she spun like a top before climbing into the cab of the truck that had come for her.

I said a prayer for her safety as the vehicle rolled away. Road conditions weren't optimal. She was young, and likely, so was her driver.

"They'll be okay," Mason said, borrowing my fork again. "I see her with that kid in that truck all the time. I ran his plates. Then his record. Nothing. No citations. Not even a speeding ticket."

I guffawed, taking the fork back. "And you called me nosy."

"I wanted to be sure she was in good hands out there," he said. "I like her."

"Me too," I said. "Thanks for looking out for her."

He angled himself to face me, far too close for my clarity of thought. "It's my job. As is solving Fryer's murder. You know whose job it isn't?"

The gruff pleading of his voice and beseeching look in his eyes turned my bones to pudding.

I felt my stiffened spine bend and my bravado fail. I knew

the answer to his question, of course. And I knew why it upset him so much to see me be threatened.

No one wanted to see someone they cared about in danger.

My thoughts raced back to a time I'd found Gigi in the hands of a killer, and my body began to respond as if that moment was happening now instead of long passed. My fingers curled, and the fork fell from my grip. My throat thickened, and my eyes blurred with unshed tears. Each pounding beat of my heart further constricted my chest.

"Bonnie?" Mason scanned me, head to toe as my breaths became shorter and more shallow.

My teeth chattered, then the tears began to fall. An indescribable charge of terror seized my every cell and fiber. I couldn't breathe. I was dying. Or maybe having a heart attack.

I clutched my chest, fighting the feelings as my body doubled down on them, skyrocketing my unincited fear.

"Hey, I've got you," Mason said, reaching for me with both arms.

I was flying. Whisked from the counter and carried like a child away from the scene of my attack.

Mason's solid, damp chest pressed against my cheek, and his strong hands held me tight. The scent of him clung to his clothes and skin, refocusing my stunned and out-of-control senses to that single sensation.

We made a loop around the counter to a display near the back corner, and he lowered me onto a velvet settee, then tipped me forward.

"Keep your head down," he said, rubbing circles on my back as he sat on the floor at my feet. "You're having a panic attack, but it'll pass. Don't be afraid of it."

I made a mental note to later tell him how stupid his advice was. It was like telling me to calm down when I was already mad. But I pinched my eyes closed and concentrated on his scent and presence, strong, steady and calm.

Time passed as I struggled to breathe. Seconds. Maybe minutes. Then the work came easier, until I no longer had to concentrate at all.

Mason kept touching me, moving his big hand in soothing strokes and circles. He used a quiet voice to tell me a story about a petting zoo from his childhood. His tone and touch helped my mind to recenter.

"So there I am," he said. "Maybe four years old, standing on the bottom rung of the petting zoo fence beside my mom with her cup of feed for llamas, and there are chickens everywhere. I thought they were funny, clucking and pecking while a woman in giant rubber boots carried a metal bucket in our direction. Then one chicken went crazy. Maybe it was just excited. I don't know, but it flew straight over the others, unsteady and bobbing. Its fat, feathered-up body and crazy hair coming straight for me."

"What?" I asked, suddenly more concerned about young Mason than the subdued ache in my chest and throat.

"It hit me," he said, gaze distant and unfocused. "It knocked me clean off the fence and into the dirt, then it doubled back, running to the feed like nothing had happened. I was left confused, hurting and with a mouth full of feathers." He turned to face me, bottom lip jutting forward. "I've still got a scar from that crazy chicken's talons. Can you see it? On the right?"

I dropped my gaze to his mouth, seeking, then finding, a noticeable groove through the smooth skin of his bottom lip. "Oh my glory."

"Right? It bled like a son of a gun," he said. "All over my shirt and hands. It throbbed and burned. Mom took me to the ER, and they put in a stitch to reduce the scarring, but it hurt more than anything that had happened to me before.

Did you know our lips are jam packed with all kinds of sensitive nerve endings?"

I felt my mouth open in response, and I lifted my eyes to his. "Yes."

He smiled. "Feeling better?"

I performed a quick internal assessment. "I think so." The words were breathless, and my heart rate was still up, but manageable, and likely increased for a completely new reason.

"I've never told anyone that petting zoo story," he said. "It's a little embarrassing, but it was for a good cause. Panic attacks are rough. I'm glad you've recovered, but you'd better take that story to your grave."

I drew a cross over my heart with one finger. "That's why you're afraid of chickens."

"I'm not afraid," he said. "I just don't like them."

"What happens when people notice the scar?" I asked. Surely plenty of people had been close enough to remark.

His mouth twitched, fighting another smile. "I tell them it was from a fist fight. That I won."

"Of course." I laughed, then slid onto the floor at his side. "Thank you for helping me."

His arm curled over my shoulders, and my head rested against him. "Always."

"I'm sorry I didn't tell you I knew about Ava sooner," I said. "It won't happen again."

"No more secrets?" he asked.

"Not big ones," I said. "There are some things that even the closest friends don't need to know."

He grunted.

"Don't be mad at Dale," I added. "He was worried, and with good reason. Plus, Cami likes him a lot, and I love Cami, so he was right the other night. We all need to get along."

"I'm not mad," he said. "I was shocked that he'd shared

something so personal, and none of his business, but I get it. I came here in a bad place. He had no idea how I was doing. Friends worry."

I liked that Mason could forgive so easily. Most people struggled with that, myself included on occasion.

"I care more about honesty than anything else," he went on, "and you were honest with me. I appreciate it. Even if it was a few months late."

I smiled. "I'll work on my timing."

The silence between us grew warm like a cocoon. The battering rain, a white-noise machine. And my previously walloping heart was at peace.

Mason took my hand in his and squeezed. "I'm sorry for what I said the other night at the lake. I shouldn't have trapped you like that. It wasn't fair, dumping my feelings on you when you had nowhere to go. I can see that now."

I straightened. Then put a few inches between us. The memory of his admission returned like an awkward shove. "It's fine. I think we've both been through some tough stuff, and what we've got going here is complicated. We probably both need to take a beat and really figure things out." Learn to trust again. Maybe teach ourselves our bad experiences were the exceptions, like Cami said, not the rule.

"Maybe," he said. "But I know what I want."

I rose to my feet, and he followed suit.

Mason widened his stance and crossed his arms to match my body language. "Let's make a deal."

"No." I shook my head. "We don't need to do that. Or talk about this. It's all fine. We're fine."

"We are." He nodded. "But we do need to talk about this. Now, hear me out." He rolled his shoulders back and tipped his head once over each shoulder, then fixed me with a determined gaze. "I won't bring the subject of us up again, until you ask me to."

"Okay," I said, dragging out the word, wondering about the catch. "And?"

"And in exchange, you're going to trust me not to have a change of heart. Because I won't. Even when you push me or challenge me. Or defy me or make me completely nuts. I'm ready, and I'm willing to wait, unless you tell me to knock it off."

I wet my lips.

"Do you want me to knock it off?"

"No," I whispered. "But could you? Knock it off?" I asked.

What he'd said was sweet, but it also felt fickle. If he was truly steadfast in his feelings for me, how could he just turn them off?

"I would work on it," he said. "If you asked. And if that's what you wanted. I would do it for you."

My heart swelled, and I heard a chunk of the protective barrier I'd built around it crack and fall. "What if I wanted to take things slowly?" I asked. "While I'm figuring out how to manage it?"

One of Mason's brows rose. "I am an incredibly patient man."

I inhaled a long steadying breath. "Okay. Then, I think we could try being something more than friends, but at a very, very slow pace. And see what happens."

His lips formed the smallest, most careful of smiles. "If that's what you want."

I unfolded my arms and stepped toward him, smile wide and ready for one of his epically perfect hugs.

He stepped forward as well and extended a hand to shake —and accidentally jammed his fingers into my cleavage.

Nope, this wouldn't be awkward at all.

CHAPTER TWENTY

*M*ason followed me to my parents' house, because there was no way I could stay at his place after the cleavage thing. And we agreed it wasn't a good idea for me to go home.

I sampled their dandelion wine over puzzles and filled them in on what I'd been up to all day. They frowned and scowled, but not at me, at whoever was threatening me. I kept the panic attack and conversation with Mason to myself. It was a small gift I planned to unpack and relive later, while trying to fall asleep.

I crawled into my childhood bed, phone in hand. Then I sent a single text to Mason.

Me: Who was with Jean on the night Fryer died?

When he didn't respond right away, I sent him the photo I'd taken earlier, of Clyde hiding beneath my ball gowns to butter him up. Because who could resist that sweet kitty face?

Then, somehow, I fell asleep, the wind howling through our old farmhouse rafters and around ancient window frames as I waited for his response.

Breakfast, however, came with a headache. I blamed the wine.

Gigi bopped through the door just in time to eat and carrying a stack of books and folders. "I'm making a business plan," she said. "I stopped by the library to read up on opening a new business and decided I'd better check out everything they had. Then I started taking notes."

I smiled. "I love a good plan."

Mom looked mildly concerned by the amount of paperwork. "I'd better make a fresh pot of coffee."

We ate inside, at the dining room table, so Gigi could spread out her books and notes. She'd printed dozens of images of other cafes and bakeries around the globe and circled all the things she liked about each of them. French provincial curtains at a patisserie in New Orleans. Vintage décor from a cider shop in West Virginia. Earthy hues and a relaxing vibe from an iced-tea shop at the seaside. I drank in the beautiful inspiration.

"I want to combine these aspects in a personal Georgia way so my bakery feels fancy and special but also as if everyone is welcome, which they are. I want folks to relax in comfort while they enjoy my sweets," Gigi said. "And I like the idea of adding throwbacks to Bliss's history with the art choices and maybe some kind of display. A little nostalgia is fun too. Those details remind me of my youth, and my mama's kitchen."

I examined the images thoroughly, then passed them down the table to Mama.

"I love all of this," Mama said.

"Me too." I smiled. "And I can help you find these décor pieces, or at least some things with equivalent appeal. We can take road trips and hit up estate sales looking for the right things."

"I'm in," she said. "For now, I'm building up my customer

base. I baked all night to make a nice selection of products. Then, I cut them all into small portions I can hand out as samples. Once I get people hooked on my goodies, they'll be lining up at my door."

Dad looked over our shoulders as he refilled our mugs with coffee, then set the carafe on the table. "What's in your business plan?"

"Oh!" Gigi perked up and grabbed the folder marked with a large scratch-and-sniff pie sticker. "I'm going to run things alone for a while," she said. "To keep costs down. I'll have limited business hours and only make as much as I think I can sell. I'll close for the day if I sell out early, and if there are leftovers, I'm donating them to the local schools. Larger cakes or pies can be gifted to the teachers' lounges, but cookies can be divvied up and sent home with the kids who get those Blessings in a Backpack." She opened her folder and riffled through the notes. "I want to host an annual bake sale to raise money for food-insufficient families in our community. And when it's time to hire help, I'll pay a fair wage."

Dad nodded, arms folded as he moved to the end of the table. "Blossom and I help fill those backpacks. It's a great initiative."

Gigi nodded. Of course, she knew how great it was to help others. Helping was the cornerstone she and Grandpa had built their life on. They'd cultivated a kind and generous heart in my mama, who'd done her best to pass those qualities on to me.

I tried to live up to my legacy, but there was always more to be done.

"I've decided to source my ingredients locally," Gigi went on. "At first I worried about how that would drive up my prices. Then I decided not to care if my goodies are a little more expensive. Because I'll know why. Spending more on quality ingredients and good help is nothing to feel bad about. Folks will understand that."

I turned on my chair and wrapped her in my arms. Gigi was so truly good and so purely invested in the well-being of others that it sometimes knocked me back a step.

She patted my back. "Well, that's enough about me for now," she said, pulling gently from my hug. "What's on your agenda for today? How's things with the HANS?"

My mind blanked at the mention of Mason. Things with him were awkward, but kind of wonderful, though a little tense, but also nice. I nearly shouted with joy when my phone rang. I'd have cheerfully talked to a stranger about my car insurance if it meant postponing my next sentence to my family. "One sec," I said, quickly answering the call. "Hello?"

"Ms. Balfour?" an unfamiliar voice asked.

"Yes."

"This is Herman Humphries from the Bliss Civil Engineers department. You left a message for one of the surveyors to return your call. That's me. What can I do for you?"

I hopped to my feet, pushing the chair back as I rose in a burst. "Of course. Thank you so much for calling."

Gigi and my parents watched me closely as I lifted a finger to indicate I'd be right back. Then, I scurried across the room so my conversation wouldn't interrupt theirs.

"What can I do for you?" Mr. Humphries asked.

"I was a friend of Mr. Fryer's," I fibbed, avoiding eye contact with my too-quiet family. "He set an appointment to meet with you, and it was important to him. I suppose you know about his death by now."

"Ah, yes," Mr. Humphries said. "A terrible thing."

"Truly," I agreed, nodding, though he couldn't see me. "What will happen now that he's gone? Will the survey be forgotten, or will you carry on as planned?"

"Without Fryer, there's really no reason," he said. "Assuming whoever inherits or buys the home doesn't have an issue with the neighbor's encroaching gardens, chickens and yard sale. I'd recommend a proper survey for the new owner, for any property owner. It makes good sense to have the boundaries marked officially. In case of future issues, like Mr. Fryer's. It's just good to know what you own. You know?"

I couldn't help wondering if I should schedule a survey for my new property, and I tucked the question into the back of my mind for later. "The scheduled survey won't move forward now?" I asked, making sure I understood clearly.

"No, ma'am. According to the file, Mr. Fryer didn't pay in advance, and I can't invoice the deceased. I hate that I wasn't able to get to that for him before he passed. He'd been so fervent, collecting evidence of the neighbor's encroachment."

"What if I paid?" I asked without thinking. I had no idea what a survey cost, but the results could be the key to Fryer's murder. "Can I do that?" I pressed when he didn't respond. "Legally, I mean."

"I suppose so," he said. "Property boundaries are a matter of public knowledge. Normally I'd say I had to ask for permission from the land owner, but he's the one who asked for the survey. If the property stakes are still in place I can locate and mark them relatively easily. I'll replace them if they're missing. The deed's available at the courthouse if you want a copy. Boundary lines are marked there as well."

"Thanks, I wouldn't have thought of that." I made a mental note to look up the deeds for Fryer's and his neighbor Alyssa's properties as soon as possible. "I'll visit the courthouse first. May I call you back if the survey is still necessary?"

"Of course. Use this number," Mr. Humphries said. "It's

my private line, and I keep it with me when I'm offsite. Which is most of the time."

We disconnected, and I turned to find both my parents and Gigi staring from their seats at the dining room table.

"I have to go," I said. "Clyde and I need to get to work. Thanks for breakfast!"

"What was that all about?" Mama asked, falling into step behind me as I headed for the cat carrier I'd left in the kitchen.

Gigi restacked her folders and books while I stuffed Clyde into his crate and kissed my parents, then she beat me to the door. "Take me with you."

Mama narrowed her eyes. "What are you two up to?"

"Nothing," Gigi and I sang in unison, rushing to my car.

"Thanks for the ride," she said. "We have to stop at my place and pick up my sample goodies."

I smiled. "Then I guess we'd better get going."

Gigi and I spent the morning volleying ideas around between customers. She'd set up a little table outside my door, just between Bless Her Heart and Blissful Bean, the site of her future bakery. She'd lined her sample goodies up for easy distribution, then bounced a few of her concerns off me as I popped out periodically to check on her. I always responded with an answer, then a question of my own.

For example, Gigi wondered if French Provincial woodwork seemed too snooty or pretentious for a Bliss bakery. And I wondered if Alyssa Sternman could've gotten the jump on Mr. Fryer in the dark.

We decided the answers were no, and yes, respectively.

French Provincial woodworking was gorgeous and anyone could appreciate its beauty without feeling threatened. Also Alyssa, or anyone else, could've gotten the jump on Fryer in the dark.

"I wish her yard sale had business hours," I said, moseying outside to lean against the wall near Gigi's table. "Assuming she's the only one who works there, it would be easy to count her out as a suspect if I knew her sale was running at the time of my threats. Can't be two places at once and all that." Believe me. I tried and failed daily. "What do we know about Alyssa Sternman?"

Gigi peered at me through wire-rimmed, heart-shaped sunglasses she'd nabbed from a rack near my counter. "I've been trying to recall why the name is so familiar, but it isn't coming to me."

I typed Alyssa's name into a search engine on my phone

Gigi pulled her phone out as well. "Let me ask Sutton. She's not in town now, and no one in Virginia will care about Bliss business. I learned my lesson asking Mirabelle."

She fixed her eyes on her phone as she typed. "Is Alyssa married to a psychiatrist?" she asked. "The one who takes appointments at his house?"

I scrunched my nose. "A yard sale doesn't seem like something a doctor would want greeting his patients."

"Maybe she was one of his patients," Gigi suggested.

I recalled the giant, ongoing, sprawling sale and wasn't sure Gigi's idea was beyond the scope of possibility. I scrolled through hundreds of articles recovered in my search. Too many to read. Too many to sort.

Something Herman Humphries, the Bliss engineer, mentioned during our call came back to me, and I rethought my strategy. Deeds were a matter of public record. So were marriage certificates and such. I could find out if Alyssa was married to a doctor with a few local searches.

I navigated to the Village of Bliss website and typed Alyssa's address into the bar made for property searches. A

few seconds later, voila! "It looks like the home was originally purchased by Dr. and Andrew Sternman," I said. "A few
years ago, there was a change, removing Andrew Sternman."

"Huh," Gigi said, setting her phone on her lap. "Was it the
year your grandpa passed?"

"Yeah."

"Oh." The sadness in her voice weighted my heart.

I kept my eyes on the phone and concentrated, willing the
familiar wave of grief to subside. "I think Alyssa was the
doctor." I plugged Andrew Sternman's name into a new
search window, followed by the words Bliss, Georgia.

An obituary appeared.

"He died," Gigi said.

"Yeah." I glanced at her unsure if she recalled the man's
death or if Sutton had responded to her text.

Gigi's shoulders drooped a bit. "I remember now. I was
packing to leave town when it happened. I was running away
from my grief, and hers was just beginning. I didn't know her
personally, but I remember the story now," she repeated.

I could tell from the pull of her lips and tilt of her brows
above the goofy glasses, the story was going to be rough. I
stepped closer, both to console her and to keep her from
having to speak more loudly than necessary, lest anyone
overhear. "Whenever you're ready," I said.

"She lost her license to practice medicine when he died,"
she said.

I gasped softly, and the conversation was stilted a
moment while Gigi delivered samples to a family passing by.

I waited impatiently for the rest. The woman who'd sold
me old books and a rusty lantern didn't fit the image I held
of a psychiatrist. Maybe there was good reason. Maybe she'd
somehow caused her husband's death, and Mr. Fryer was the
second man in her life who'd provoked her deadly ire.

I turned my focus back to the phone screen while Gigi

talked with a pair of women arriving on the family's heels. I plugged combinations of Alyssa and Andrew Sternmans' names into my phone, along with words like *death* and *accused*, until I'd gathered enough information to understand why.

She had been accused of his death, or at least of contributing to it.

Gigi waved me close as the group cleared away from her goodies table. "Her husband was injured in a farming accident shortly after they married, and he needed around-the-clock care. That was why she'd begun seeing patients at their home. I got the story twisted in my head," she said. "They were so young. It was awful. He was in a lot of pain, and they thought he'd never walk again. He did eventually, but the recovery was rough. Folks said she cracked one night and prescribed him pills to help with the pain when his physicians had cut him off."

I felt my mouth form a little o. "She wasn't supposed to do that." She wasn't that kind of doctor, and she should never have prescribed anything for her husband.

"He got hooked," Gigi said. "Eventually, he overdosed, and the whole thing came out."

A gust of air blew from my lungs, and I saw Alyssa in a completely new light. Her radical yard sale suddenly seemed more reasonable. Because I had no idea how I would cope with the past she'd lived through. "How did I never know that?" In a town that knew when, where and how hard I stubbed my toe, it was tough to fathom how something this huge had never crossed my ears. His death had been a few years before my return, but I'd been back a year now and heard plenty of less substantial gossip.

"I suppose, in some ways," Gigi said, "we don't talk about it because we all wonder if we might've done the same thing in her shoes. I know I would do anything to help a loved one in pain. If I lived with them and their pain around the clock, if I was young and grieving my husband's possible permanent loss of mobility with him, if I was a psychiatrist with little life experience and my love was in horrendous pain..." She shook her head, and I imagined her eyes glistening with unshed tears behind the glasses. "I think she acted out of desperation and misguided love. I don't blame her for the mistake she made, and I doubt anyone regrets those decisions more than she does."

I nodded and turned my eyes away.

I'd never experienced a love or a loss like that. I had, however, watched my grandpa's death turn my peppy, bright-eyed grandma into a shell before she ran away to a naturalist commune for several years. I understood that heartbreak made sensible people do out-of-character things.

"I suppose the yard sale is her main source of income now," Gigi said. "That and whatever she and her husband saved before his death."

"What about life insurance?" I asked.

Gigi lifted and lowered one shoulder in a weak shrug. "Maybe. I don't know the family or if they had more money than most, but I'm guessing Andrew racked up some heavy medical bills following that accident. Enough to take a toll on most."

So, when Fryer started pushing back against her yard sale —her only known source of income and possibly a well-established coping mechanism—how far would she have gone to stop him?

CHAPTER TWENTY-ONE

*C*lyde and I slept at my place that night, with a deputy on patrol outside. He was nice enough to knock on our door shortly after we'd arrived home, introduce himself as Deputy Frond, and let us know what he was up to. Apparently, the good sheriff had asked him to keep a lookout until his shift ended. Another deputy would take over from there, but wouldn't, according to Frond, knock on my door. Presumably because the next deputy's shift would begin after I'd gone to bed.

Frond had been too tight-lipped to tell me where the sheriff was and what he was up to. Or why, if Mason thought my personal protection was necessary, had he turned to smoke instead of guarding me himself.

I'd checked my phone throughout the night, expecting to hear from Mason, but I did not, and I was too stubborn to message him. I'd been the last one to text, after all.

And all I got was silence.

My messages were marked as read, so it wasn't as if he didn't receive them.

"And that is what burns my biscuits," I told Clyde in the morning as I adjusted his debonair paisley bow tie. "Mason professes his feelings for me, insists we can take it as slowly as I want, then he vanishes." I performed my most shocked expression. "In case he doesn't understand, this is not an example of letting me control the pace. In fact, this is an excellent example of how to scare me away before our first kiss."

The thought of kissing Mason stunned me silent for a long beat. We were officially taking things slowly, but kissing was coming. Kissing is what people who had feelings for one another did.

So there would be kissing.

I probably shouldn't be nervous, considering he'd already gotten to second base with that cleavage incident.

I carried Clyde into the hallway and faced the massive framed mirror I'd leaned against the wall for dramatic flair.

"What do we think?" I asked Clyde. "Pretty snazzy, right?"

I'd paired a sleeveless silk blouse the color of coffee creamer with an ice-blue cashmere cardigan and finished the outfit with black slacks. The slacks did nice things for my derriere, and I wished I owned ten pairs.

Clyde's pale-blue-and-white bow tie coordinated perfectly and stood out well against his sleek black fur.

He headed for his carrier when I set him down, ready to start the day.

I took a moment to admire the work I'd done before bed, and enjoyed the deep sense of satisfaction that came with my view. Local crews had done a lovely job refinishing my floors and revamping the home's layout. They'd installed my kitchen cabinets and backsplash. I'd painted the walls earlier this week, and all that had been left to do last night was decorate. So, for the first time in years, I'd cleared my busy mind with interior design instead of baking. The results were impressive, even to my own eyes.

The light, airy color scheme went well with my lake-front location. Careful pops of navy, aqua, peach and pink completed the look and made me smile. Best of all, I'd done it on a shoestring budget and helped others in the process.

I grabbed my phone, keys and purse, then swiped Clyde's carrier from the floor. Today was a good day.

I waved to the new deputy on duty as I pulled out of my driveway and felt a twinge of guilt for not offering him anything for breakfast or at least a cup of coffee. He'd spent his entire shift so far looking after me, and it seemed the least I could do in return.

Cold wind ruffled the remaining leaves on nearby trees. Thankfully, the marshmallow's heater warmed me through by the time I reached the end of my road.

My phone dinged in the cup holder as I slowed at the stop sign, and Mason's number appeared onscreen.

I checked my rearview mirror to confirm no one was behind me, then I checked the message.

Mason: Tom

My phone dinged again before I could ask him to elaborate.

Mason: I'll meet you at your shop in an hour

I frowned for a long moment before I understood. The last thing I'd asked Mason was who Jean was with on the night Mr. Fryer died. Mason had said earlier that she'd been with another member of the Road Crew, but he hadn't told me which one

She'd been with Tom. AKA Axel. AKA the man Fryer had lowballed in his time of need.

My hands trembled as I typed my single letter response, then set the phone back in my cup holder.

Me: K

The man providing Jean's alibi for the night of Mr. Fryer's death was another one of my suspects?

Did that mean both had alibis now or neither?

I crawled along the roads toward downtown, distracted and contemplating.

I pulled over when a blue-and-white van in a nearby driveway caught my eye. The logo for a local home-security company covered the door, and my intuition spiked.

At first, I wasn't sure why. Then, Herman Humphries's voice returned to me. The village surveyor had said he regretted not being able to perform Mr. Fryer's property survey, because Fryer had been adamant about collecting information on his neighbor's encroachment. At the time I'd assumed Mr. Fryer had meant the survey, but what if Mr. Fryer had been monitoring his property line some other ways as well?

I pulled back into traffic and changed directions. It was a long shot, but I had a while before Mason expected me at work, and Fryer's place was only seven minutes away. I could do a quick drive by and still get to Bless Her Heart before Mason.

A shot of adrenaline jolted through my veins as I motored toward my new destination.

Part of me suspected Mason would've already thought of this, but the rest of me needed to see for myself.

My phone rang as I approached my destination. I pulled onto the driveway outside Mr. Fryer's home. Alyssa's driveway, only a few feet away, already had a couple cars in it, possibly waiting for her big sale.

I cringed at the sight of Mason's face on my screen.

"Hello?" I answered, climbing out and watching as Alyssa dragged furniture onto her lawn.

She was certainly dedicated to her task.

"Everything okay?" Mason asked without preamble. "I

thought I saw your car pull over in the middle of traffic headed downtown."

"I'm fine," I assured, wondering how I'd missed him if he'd passed me on the street. Maybe I'd been more distracted than I'd realized.

"No car trouble?"

"No." I turned in a small circle, feeling a little as if I was being watched. Deciding there was likely an onlooker at Alyssa's sale, I headed for Mr. Fryer's porch, peering over the flimsy yellow crime-scene tape. "If you thought I had car trouble, why didn't you stop to help or call me sooner?"

"Because," he grouched. "I was on my way to the court-house, and I didn't have time to stop. Besides, I figured if you had car trouble on a road with plenty of passersby, at least you'd be safe until I came back out. You weren't there. So, what are you up to?"

"Why were you in a hurry to get to the courthouse?" I asked, dodging his question and hoping for information to soothe my curious mind.

"You first."

I looked around, debating how to best answer and in no mood to be scolded.

"You can do it," he said, voice low and enticing. "Tell me yours and I'll tell you mine."

I explained my theory about the security cameras as I circled the house, checking Fryer's windows and lawn for signs he paid a security company. There weren't any.

Across the grass, early birds inspected Alyssa's wares.

"Fryer didn't have a home security system and neither does Sternman," Mason said. "Are you headed to work now, or should I meet you there?"

I checked the time on my watch. I had time before I needed to open my shop, but I was admittedly intrigued by Mason's trip to the courthouse and the related news he'd yet to share. "I'm on my way downtown," I said. "Meet you at the shop in fifteen minutes?"

"Yep."

I disconnected and strode across the backyard, chin held high. I slowed when a chicken crossed my path and promptly pooed on Fryer's cobblestone patio, then clucked away.

I grimaced, understanding how that could've been frustrating.

A shadow fell across the grass and stretched toward me. I froze as Alyssa Sternman marched my way. "Is it true?" she called, clutching and tightening a large pashmina around her hunched shoulders. "Are you paying to have this property surveyed? Even after Fryer is gone?"

I backed up a step, intimidated by her heated tone and purposeful stride. "Where did you hear that?" I asked, hoping to turn the accusation into a conversation and also that she would settle down. I checked our immediate surroundings for anything she might use as a weapon.

"I heard it straight from Herman Humphries!" she shouted, her gaunt face contorted with rage. "Why would you do that? Why? Why!"

I stumbled over a chicken, barely catching the handrail to Fryer's rear porch before falling over.

She narrowed her gaze on me, and music blasted suddenly, turning her in the direction of her yard. "Turn it down!" she yelled. "There's a noise ordinance!"

I took several big steps away while she dithered, torn between reducing the volume on the radio and laying into me further.

Eventually, she huffed and jogged back toward her home. "We're not finished!" she yelled over her shoulder as she stormed away.

I moved immediately in the opposite direction, ready to meet Mason before I became the next body on Fryer's porch.

The world went dark as I rounded the corner, heading back toward my car. Something rough, like an empty feed sack, had been pulled low over my head, and a pair of strong arms circled my middle.

"You're coming with me," a low, husky voice whispered. "And you're going for your last ride."

CHAPTER TWENTY-TWO

I screamed.

The assailant lifted my feet from the ground, and I kicked.

"Help!" I wailed and flailed, but the bag muffled my cries.

The music volume lowered next door, and I suddenly suspected the person who'd nabbed me was the one who'd cranked it up.

"Let me go!" I screeched, hoping to be heard across the yards and through the home at my side.

My would-be abductor huffed and grunted, struggling to drag me in what I presumed was the direction of my last ride.

I alternated my defense, kicking wildly until my feet connected with the ground, then digging in my heels.

My attacker's determined grunts quickly turned to whispered curses, and I realized my attacker wasn't a man.

I'd put on some weight over the years, but I still wouldn't have been any match for Tom, AKA Axel, AKA the only male on my pitiful suspect list.

Whoever was trying to drag me away was much taller

than Alyssa or Vivian. So, unless Fryer's killer was someone I hadn't thought of, I knew exactly who this was.

"Jean?"

My captor stilled, and her grip softened marginally.

I rammed my elbows back like my life depended on it and lurched away.

The bag clung to my face as I heaved for air, stumbling blindly forward and tugging the material away to free my eyes.

"Help!" I screamed, renewing the campaign. "Help!"

Jean caught me again and yanked me sideways, tossing me into Fryer's garage.

My arms pinwheeled as I bumbled through the utility door before Jean slammed the barrier closed behind us.

She swept a tire iron off a work bench and raised it over her head.

I flipped my palms up as I inched backward, surveying our new surroundings and putting as much space between Jean and me as possible.

Her toe collided with something metal, sending the item skittering across the smooth cement floor. Her gaze followed the movement, and I darted around the hood of an old red pickup truck.

"Why are you doing this?" I asked, scents of motor oil and metal crept into my nose. "Stop," I pleaded. "Talk to me. We can clear things up."

Jean blinked, appearing bewildered by a situation she'd created. Her mouth opened and shut like a fish out of water. Her eyes were red and puffy. She clearly didn't have a plan. "Why did you have to get involved in this?" she croaked. "I had it handled. It was going to be fine."

I felt my features instinctively bunch, and a sarcastic response tumbled out of me. *"Fine."*

She narrowed her wide eyes, apparently catching my drift.

Was killing an old man really ever going to be fine? Was threatening me at every turn? Or murdering me in cold blood?

Nothing about those things was fine.

"So judgy," she snipped. "So righteous. Little Miss Perfect with your colorful clothes and peppy personality."

I frowned. "You don't like my clothes or personality?"

Her gaze darkened. "This was supposed to be between me and Hotrod, but you had to get involved. You had to come to his house that night. Had to show up at his shop the next day. Then at Crossroads. Now you're here again. You're like a bad rash," she griped. "You just won't go away."

I tucked myself behind the truck a little farther, wondering how late I had to be for Mason to come looking for me. "Careful," I warned when she stepped closer. "At least put the weapon down. You don't want to accidentally scratch or hurt this truck. Even if it was Fryer's."

"It. Wasn't. Fryer's. Truck!" she yelled, biting out each word. "This is Axel's truck. Axel's. Not Hotrod's. He basically stole it, and I've been trying to get it back."

I gave the truck a cursory look, careful to keep the unhinged woman six feet away. "You committed murder over a truck?"

"It was an accident," she seethed. "I tried to reason with an unreasonable old tool, and I lost!" Her eyes went gonzo, and spittle flew from her lips. "First, I tried using my feminine wiles, which had suited him just fine before, but he told me to go home as soon as I brought up the truck."

She stepped closer, and I stepped back, edging around the rearview mirror.

On the wall beside me, a dimly lit button caught my eye.

A garage door opener.

"I came here to talk to him," she said. "Axel is my friend, and what Hotrod did to him was ruthless. I wanted him to fix things before the trouble he'd caused broke up the whole club. Axel was going to leave the Road Crew. If he did, I knew some of the others would've gone with him." She pressed her lips. "That club is my life. They treat me like I matter. They're always glad to see me. Not like when I'm at work, being actively ignored and excluded. Auto shops are a total guys' club. Don't let anyone tell you different. And being ignored hurts."

I knew a thing or two about being ignored. I'd endured it far too long, but I'd been married.

I couldn't help wondering why Jean had chosen a workplace and club where she wasn't fully embraced. Surely there were other auto shops where she could work. And clubs like the Road Crew that allowed female members.

I wanted to ask why she'd never considered starting a group or garage of her own, but I suspected this wasn't the time. And that I already knew the answer.

No one had ever taught Jean that she had power. The power to grow and change, to leave bad situations and create better ones. She didn't have a cheering section like mine. No Mama and Dad telling her whatever she chose to do would be supported fully. No Gigi, prepared to fight the good fight, whatever battle she entered. No Cami listening to her cry over things she couldn't change, while not judging her desire to stay where she was a little longer.

And my heart broke anew.

"I'm so sorry," I said, then lunged toward the wall, slapping the rectangular button.

The large door behind me began to rise.

Jean squinted against the flood of light. She dove around the truck's hood, but I was already on the move.

I ducked under the door as it made its slow ascent, a cry for help dying on my tongue.

"Jeanette Marie Rikers," Mason bellowed, his purposeful strides eating up the lawn, one hand on his sidearm, clearly prepared to draw if needed. "You are under arrest for the murder of Joseph Fryer, unlawful entry of The Truck Stop, threatening and terrorizing Bonnie Balfour, and I'm guessing her abduction and attempted murder as well."

Jean froze at my side, the tire iron falling from her hand.

The deputy I recognized from outside my home this morning read her her rights.

I launched myself at Mason.

He kissed my hair, my cheeks and nose. "Sorry I'm late," he said, resting his forehead against mine. "You okay?"

I nodded, speechless but trembling.

Mason's filthy Jeep sat haphazardly behind the marshmallow, as if he'd torn onto the property and leaped out while the vehicle was still moving. The deputy's cruiser was on the street at the edge of Fryer's lawn.

Jean's multicolored car was barely visible in the distance, tucked covertly against a nearby tree line. And I realized the car would've been nearly invisible there at night.

"How'd you know I was still here?" I asked, ignoring the line of rubberneckers leering from Alyssa Sternman's driveway.

He tipped his head toward the deputy sliding cuffs on Jean's wrists. "Deputy Mars followed you when you left home this morning. He called and offered to keep watch outside your shop until I could pick up the warrant I'd requested from Judge Hassle, who is aptly named, by the way." Mason rolled his eyes and stroked my hair, examining me for signs of injury. "I planned to search Jean's dad's auto shop for a specific color paint used on a make of cars from the early last century. I planned to fill you in on things when you got to your shop, then make my arrest before dinner."

"But I didn't go to work."

He shook his head. "Nope. And neither did Jean. Thankfully, Mars got out to take a look when you didn't come back around the house after a few minutes. I was already planning to arrest her, while trying to protect you, and the two of you wound up in one place, with a deputy on your heels. I gave the warrant for the auto shop to Frond, but I'm guessing your statement will confirm my suspicions."

"She confessed to Fryer's murder," I said. "But I think his death was an accident, and it'll be her word against mine in court."

"I'm building a nice case," Mason said. "You always underestimate me."

I smiled, because that was an absolutely crazy statement. "Tell me about the paint. Was it found at the crime scene?"

Mason glanced around, then angled himself away from the crowd. "No, but it was found on one of the carvings your cat stole."

I frowned. "I thought the bag of figures was missing."

"It was," he said. "But…" He fished his phone from his pocket and tapped the screen, then turned it to face me.

The image of Clyde I'd sent him last night looked back.

I smiled. "He's so handsome."

Mason used his thumb and forefinger to increase the size of the image, until I noticed the top of a miniature clock tower poking out from beneath one of Clyde's rear paws. "On the day Fryer's body was found, you showed me a photo of all the pieces you returned to him. The clock tower was one of them. It wouldn't make sense to carve more than one of any particular shop, so I guessed this was one of the ones in the earlier photo."

"You think Clyde stole it a second time?"

"Yep."

"How?" I asked, sweeping my gaze to the porch beside us. "Clyde couldn't possibly have come all the way to Fryer's home alone." And he definitely couldn't have carried a miniature clock tower all the way downtown.

"He didn't have to come here, if the killer took the bag of figures somewhere closer," Mason said.

"Like The Truck Stop."

Mason nodded. "You said it yourself. Jean was hanging around the square. I think she was looking for the title to her friend's truck, but I'm not sure. I'll know more when I question her."

"What about the paint?"

"If she kept the bag of figures with her, she could've dropped one, or spilled the bag at work." He shrugged. "I'll ask. It was a hunch and a work in progress."

I considered this, piecing the puzzle together slowly. "So, you used the key I gave you on the night of the storm to go back and look for the carving."

"It was still lying there," Mason said. "Under the ball gowns, just like in the picture. I had the lab test it for something that could lead me to the killer."

"And they found paint."

He smiled. "The wood absorbed a bit of Andalusite Blue. One of only four color choices used on the original Model A Ford."

"A classic car," I said. "Like the ones worked on at her place of business. That's impressive."

"I keep trying to tell you," he said. "I'm really good at my job."

"I can't believe Clyde solved another investigation."

Mason's expression turned painfully bland. "Your cat would be in jail for kleptomania if he was a human."

"You'd have to catch him first." I stepped away to check on the kitty in my car.

Mason followed.

"You sure you aren't hurt?" he asked.

"Yep."

Clyde was fast asleep in a shaft of sun through the window.

I wound my arms around Mason's middle and snuggled against his chest as Jean was helped into the back of the deputy's cruiser. "None of this should've happened," I said. "I think she just needed a friend."

He held me while the cruiser pulled away and disappeared into traffic. "You have a big heart, Bonnie Balfour. But we've got to work on your sleuthing addiction."

CHAPTER TWENTY-THREE

Two Weeks Later

Mason met me at work on the night of my official housewarming party. My folks and Gigi had been at my place all afternoon, cooking, cleaning and setting up outdoor seating with heaters. I'd finally purchased patio furniture and borrowed dozens of folding chairs.

"Ready?" I asked, stepping onto the sidewalk and waiting for my date to join me.

Brisk autumn air whipped around us, setting my hair aloft and chilling my neck above my coat collar. I'd paired jeans and booties with a cable-knit sweater and wool coat for the evening. There would be heaters under the tents, but as the hostess, I would have to keep moving.

"Ready," Mason said. He'd tucked Clyde and his carrier under one arm and gathered a set of large shopping bags in his fingertips.

I'd filled the shopping bags with smaller bags and closed each of those with a bow. Inside were handmade bookmarks and tokens from my shop along with cookies made by Gigi. I planned to hand the bags out at my party.

I rose onto my toes to kiss Mason's cheek. He looked impossibly more handsome in the twinkling light from my display window.

The light also illuminated my new white window cling, which proudly announced Bless Her Heart as winner of the inaugural storefront decorating contest.

"What was that for?" Mason asked, leading me to his Jeep and opening the door with a grin.

I used my thumb to brush invisible lipstick from his skin, a wonderful excuse for touching him. "I don't know," I said. "I've had a good day, and I kind of like you, I guess."

He tucked my things and Clyde into the back seat before leveling me with his most smoldering stare. "You guess?"

"Kind of," I whispered as he leaned closer.

"I'm going to have to work on that."

He released me from his stare and moved around to the driver's side.

I collapsed onto my seat. "You washed your Jeep," I said, surprised at how white the paint was without the usually present dirt and mud.

"Big night," he said, smiling as he pulled away from the curb.

We rode in companionable silence over winding country roads toward Cromwell Lake and the party awaiting me. Only the suit hanging in the back window gave away the kind of day he might've had.

"Go on," Mason said, giving me significant side eye. "Ask."

"How were things in court?"

Jean had pleaded guilty on lesser charges in hope of a lighter sentence, and Mason had gone to see that Judge

Hassle had all the facts and information he needed. I'd been exceedingly kind while giving my statement following the botched abduction, but she needed to face the things she'd done. Including the murder of Joe Fryer.

"She's never been in trouble before," he said. "And there's no question of premeditation. She'll do time, but she's an engaged and active member of her community. That man, Tom, from the Road Crew testified on her behalf," Mason continued, shooting me a curious look. "He said she was kind and generous. A good friend who'd taken a wrong turn and hadn't been able to find her way back."

I nodded. That sounded right to me. "She'd been trying to help him get his truck back. That's how this all started."

Mason reached for my hand and twined his fingers with mine. "You know what else happened?"

"What?"

"After the trial, I saw an attorney greet Tom outside the courtroom. She said someone hired her to look into his child-custody situation."

"Is that right?" I said, moving my gaze to the beautiful night beyond my window.

Mason lifted our joined hands and pressed a kiss on my knuckles. "What do you think of that?"

I smiled. "I hope things work out for him. He seems like a good man."

We took the final turn onto my street a few moments later, then, as was becoming his habit, Mason veered into a field and shifted into park.

"What are you doing?" I asked, only mildly startled.

"I thought you might want a minute to breathe before we put our party faces on."

He climbed out and rounded the front of his Jeep to my door.

I accepted his offered hand and we climbed onto the hood.

We sat shoulder to shoulder in the cool darkness, his arm looped around my back.

Stars twinkled overhead, and water lapped in the distance, much like the night he'd first told me he cared for me. The night he'd promised we could take things as slow as I needed, and that I could trust him not to leave.

"Thanks for this," I said, snuggling a little more deeply against his side. "I needed this, but I also can't wait to get home."

"Quite the conundrum."

I snorted. "Shut up. I have a surprise waiting for you at my place."

Mason straightened. "Yeah?"

"Yep."

He slid to his feet in the grass and turned to face me. For the first time, I was taller.

"What's the surprise?" he asked, not looking especially curious. His gaze fell to my mouth, and he stepped closer, lifting my hands and setting them behind his neck.

"Well," I said, a bit more breathy than necessary. "I can tell you, but first you'll have to kiss me."

His brows rose by a fraction, and his hands immediately cupped my cheeks.

Mason pressed his warm, yielding mouth to mine, and I melted into the pure magic of his kiss.

I almost didn't have the heart to tell him about my surprise.

The Good Luck Falls calendars were in.

THANK YOU SO MUCH FOR READING BEATING THE WRAP! I HOPE YOU'LL ENJOY EACH NEW STORY IN THE BONNIE & CLYDE MYSTERIES MORE THAN THE LAST AND THAT YOU'LL KEEP IN TOUCH BETWEEN THE BOOKS!

Don't forget to pick up your FREE copy of
How Bonnie Met Clyde (A Prequel),
exclusively at:
https://www.julieannelindsey.com

I HOPE YOU'LL TAKE A MOMENT TO LEAVE A REVIEW IF YOU ENJOYED THIS STORY. REVIEWS ARE AUTHOR-GOLD AND SO APPRECIATED!

And if you're ready for the next Bonnie & Clyde adventure, you can order Eyelet Witness now!

ABOUT THE AUTHOR

Julie Anne Lindsey is an award-winning and bestselling author of mystery and romantic suspense. She's published more than forty novels since her debut in 2013 and currently writes series as herself, as well as under the pen names **Bree Baker**, **Jacqueline Frost**, and **Julie Chase**.

When Julie's not creating new worlds or fostering the epic love of fictional characters, she can be found in Kent, Ohio, enjoying her blessed Midwestern life. And probably plotting murder with her shamelessly enabling friends. Today she hopes to make someone smile. One day she plans to change the world.

ALSO BY JULIE ANNE LINDSEY

Bonnie & Clyde Mysteries

Eyelet Witness (Book 4 of 8)

Patience Price Mysteries

Murder by the Seaside (Book 1 of 4)

Seaside Cafe Mysteries

Live & Let Chai (Book 1 of 7)

Cider Shop Mysteries

Apple Cider Slaying (Book 1 of 3)

Christmas Tree Farm Mysteries

Twelve Slays of Christmas (Book 1 of 3)

Kitty Couture Mysteries

Cat Got Your Diamonds (Book 1 of 4)

Made in the USA
Las Vegas, NV
06 April 2022

46968739R00121